THE
MORTICIAN

COPYRIGHT DISCLAIMER

A NOVEL

BY
A. L.
MENGEL

A NOTE FROM THE AUTHOR

To My Beloved Friends of '*The Writing Studio*',

This novel has proven one of the most difficult I have ever written. There were many times, during the writing of this novel, where I busied myself with other things. It could have been research, or listening to music. Tending to the yard, or the little intricacies of life. Because of that, this book took far longer to write than I had anticipated, and the release date was moved several times.

What I think may have been happening was my subconscious mind separating itself from the work. No one, including myself, really wants to die. It's just an unfortunate fact of life that we all must deal with at some point. But when I was researching and writing about Morticians, Funeral Homes, and all of the practices of sorrow, grieving and burial, I took pause.

I wasn't necessarily 'stalling' while writing this book. During the breaks I took, I was simply stepping back into life. I did things that were a reaffirmation of life, regardless of whether I realized I was doing them or not. Because, while writing this book, that reaffirmation of life was profoundly important.

Researching and writing about death is not for everyone. But still, even with the challenges surrounding the topic, I was presented with another challenge: to make the story entertaining, but not depressing.

I was very distracted when writing this story. It's the most distracted I had ever been writing any book. And I know that these days we live in a distracted world. The Internet and Facebook have proven to be wonderfully valuable tools for the Independent Author, and Traditionally Published Author alike. Of course, there are numerous posts in online writers' groups poking fun at Authors who spend hours in online chat forums as opposed to working on their novel. But those are a necessary evil. Connections are made, readers are found, and Authors can achieve their dreams via social media. I've been fairly active in the online community, which has helped nurture my own writing career towards growth.

Still, there comes a time when a writer must buckle down and complete the project and see it to completion. Blaming Facebook, Twitter and Social Media in general makes an easy scapegoat. Still, I had challenges with this project. And I don't believe that Social Media was to blame. In retrospect, I really think it had to do with the subject matter: who wants to face death? We'd rather not deal with it until we have to, right?

But I did. I sat down, did the research, and got the story written, although it took me far longer than I had anticipated or planned for. The originally scheduled release date for this novel was October 31, 2017. When the first teaser trailer released in the end of 2016, the

October date was promoted. Parchman's Press had envisioned a grand Halloween release for a book that was dark, scary, and mysterious.

In the summer of 2017, however, things took a different turn. Research had begun back in spring of 2017, but production had started painfully slow, and the project was already weeks behind. So it was decided to move the date to December 19, 2017. As I sit here writing this, we're still in late November 2017. But what's really amazing about this book is the journey that it took me on while writing it. I discovered that this isn't really a horror story. Sure, there are scary sequences. But all in all, I found it's a story of legacy. And what we leave behind. And hopefully, it will take some of the fear *out* of death, rather than inserting more fear *about* death, as so many horror stories do.

And now, without further ado, let's let the horror continue…

A.L.

THE
BOOKSHELF

FROM THE TALES OF TARTARUS

Ashes

The Quest for Immortality

The Blood Decanter

War Angel

FROM THE VEGA CHRONICLES

The Wandering Star

The Europa Effect

OTHER WORKS

Curtains and Fan Blades

#Writestorm

The Other Side of the Door

Ashes Special Hardcover Edition

IN-DEPTH
REVIEWS FOR THE
TALES OF
TARTARUS

"Ashes touches on some pretty deep issues that are prevalent in the world today – characters struggle with sexual identity, depression and anger, intolerance and bigotry, alcoholism, drug abuse and domestic battery. "It's really a sad story," Mengel said. "It does offer hope, though. Hope for forgiveness. We all are sinners, we are all imperfect. But the cleansing act of forgiveness – the power of that simple act is shown tremendously in this story."

– via AMAZON

THE QUEST
FOR IMMORTALITY

"The Quest for Immortality examines one of the most profound issues in society today, in the traditions of Greek Mythology and the story of Narcissus. A tale of self-admiration and over indulgence, the hero of the story, Darius, is a man who was once immortal, and has lost his gift of immortality. His body is aging rapidly and he is preparing to die. It's certainly a tale 'of luxuriant wickedness'. Not for the faint of heart."

– via BARNES AND NOBLE

THE BLOOD
DECANTER

"A brilliant tour-de-force through the psyche of immortals. The series is akin to a Bildungsroman for the character Antoine, made more interesting by the intricate and non-chronological manner in which the story is presented. A.L. Mengel touches on such dichotomies as human agency as opposed to predestination, the role of nature vs. nurture in the development of a person, and redemption contrasted with damnation." – via AMAZON

War Angel

"War Angel is a fascinating stand-alone story; those readers who have enjoyed previous books in The Tales of Tartarus will be delighted by the brilliant scenarios used by the author to bring the entire series together. I, for one, hope that A.L.Mengel will someday soon gift his readers with another novel that is as captivating, entertaining, imaginative and powerful as War Angel. There are times when we all need a war angel in our lives."

— *via* AMAZON

READ EXCERPTS FROM EACH NOVEL AT THE END OF THE BOOK

From the world of The Tales of Tartarus — When the offices of The Astral's Paranormal Investigations Unit were destroyed, their files were stolen.

When they were recovered, the content was examined and analyzed in detail.

Here are the stories found inside…

THE
ASTRAL
FILES

BOOK ONE

THE
MORTICIAN

The Narrator of

The Tales of Tartarus

THE
MORTICIAN

FOR MOM

The one who taught me that the body is temporary but the soul is forever

Miss you Grandma, and Grandma, and Grandpa, and Grandpa.

See you all on the other side.

STEEL TEARS

In the middle of my sorrow, you light the way,

Always there to light the way for me.

Guiding me past the darkness,

And opening my eyes to clarity.

Though my sight is hindered by tears,

Brought on by the weight of these hurts and fears.

And all I put into those many years,

All I have left now are these steel tears.

\-   Shane Chase

DEARLY
DEPARTED

Our Death Is Our Wedding With Eternity —

RUMI

JUST DAYS BEFORE HIS THIRTIETH BIRTHDAY, and nearly twenty-seven years *after* it happened, Jacob Benjamin could still remember standing on the stepstool next to his Grandmother's coffin.

He clutched his blankie in his small, determined hands, and looked at Gramma. Her eyes were closed; there was a slight smile on her face, but it was just that – slight.

She looked like she was sleeping.

Was she going to wake up?

Despite the passage of time, his mind had still painted a perfect picture: as if she were the subject of an oil painting. A sleeping beauty of sorts. And when he remembered the scene over two decades later, he knew, that when he had stood on the step stool as a small child, all he wondered about was when Gramma was going to wake up and do the choo-choo.

As he remembered the visual of her body in the casket, he reminisced every tiny detail, as if each tiny detail of the scene before him were a specific and determined stroke of the brush; and the crimson tinged palette before him was noted despite his young age: it had been an artful presentation.

She was a sleeping beauty surrounded by white lilies and roses, bathed in a rose tinted light. An equally warm look to her skin. He hadn't known, in those days, that it was the makeup and creams that added a more lifelike appearance.

That the formaldehyde which was pumped into her veins was tinted to make it appear as if she were still alive.

But he knew it twenty-seven years after the viewing when he stood on the stepstool next to the casket as a three year old little boy.

Nor had he known that the tint applied to the lightbulbs on the standing lamps on either side of the coffin actually had a purpose: to make her skin look like blood had still flowed through her dead veins.

But twenty seven years later, he knew the purpose of the hue of the lamps.

Her body lay meticulously in the center of the casket, surrounded by soft, supple, creamy satin. The lid was propped open. Her face had a peaceful expression; as if she were sleeping, as if she had just dozed off, perhaps while watching television, or after a shared family meal, or board games with the children.

Her mouth had a slight smile; not overly so, but a subtle translation of euphoria. But there was not the slightest depiction that she was anything other than a sleeping beauty.

He looked at her lifeless, yet peaceful looking body, lying in the middle of a sea of cream colored satin, underneath a golden hanging crucifix, which was nestled in the center of the pleats of satin on the propped open lid.

She could have been merely sleeping. In her elegant surroundings. That was all, really.

Just sleeping.

On display for everyone to see, but simply off in dreamland, and she certainly was going to awake at any time, sit up, and ask everyone why they were so somber and dressed in dark suits.

Although he was still a toddler when his grandmother had passed, the memories were still vivid, as if the funeral had been just yesterday. The sweet, wafting smoke of the incense still rose into the air and the perfumed smell of the flowers flowed through his nostrils as he inhaled; he could still hear the muffled conversations at the viewing, and he could still remember the cold, firm feel to her cheek after he had touched it with his finger. And the organ was playing in the background. Then, to him, it just sounded like music. And twenty-seven later, he still did not know the name of the hymn.

But when he gazed upon Gramma, he could remember, even at his young, tender age, the days when she would carry him in her heavy arms. When she would cook him dinners that only a Gramma could make. But the thoughts that swam through his mind swirled with ferocity: she just *had* to be asleep. He didn't know the answers to the questions that added in number: why wouldn't she wake up?

He leaned on the edge of the casket, his brown penny loafers falling off his heels as he placed his weight on his toes. He could feel the cool air through his thin black dress socks. He turned and looked around the room.

Mommy and Daddy were talking.

He turned and looked at Gramma again. And then he reached out with a pointed index finger, slowly, and lightly touched her cheek.

He gasped and drew his finger back quickly. His face fell, his mouth agape, his small, wide child eyes open and wondering.

He turned around and saw Mother and Father standing nearby, hugging some other adults, their eyes red rimmed, tears streaming down their faces.

"Mommy?"

She released her friend, who dabbed at her eyes with a tissue. Mommy opened her eyes and looked down at her young son. She held a wadded up tissue near her cheek and tilted her head to the side.

Her voice was soft and defeated. She leaned down closer to him and whispered into his ear.

"What is it, Jacob?"

He frowned but his eyes remained wide. "Mommy? Gramma won't wake up...she keeps *sleeping*..."

Mommy covered her mouth with the tissue and closed her eyes.

She bent over and picked him up, but he kept looking at gramma, lying in the casket, her hands folded at her waist, holding a small, black Rosary.

"But she's so *cold* mommy!"

Even after the passage of time, he still remembered the bite of the wind against his face as he stood in the dim, grey February afternoon under a blanket of clouds and snow flurries. His father's hand felt so big, wrapped around his hand. His fingers felt warm in his tiny, knitted mittens, and his Father's fingers held tight as they enveloped his little hand as they watched the funeral motorcade approach the vestibule of the church.

At the beginning of the procession was a long Cadillac limousine, which pulled off to the side. The driver, dressed completely in black, rushed to the back door and opened it. He saw his grandpa step out.

And then Jacob turned and looked at the other cars which approached the doors. A black hearse followed the limousine, and pulled up right in front of where they stood, waiting.

Small puffs of white vapor flowed across the chill of the air as they breathed.

Jacob saw the brown casket inside through the side windows. He recognized the white flowers from the funeral home last night.

He tugged at his father's coat lapel.

He could still remember the look on his daddy's face when he looked down at him. His eyes, red-rimmed, puffy. "What is it, tyke?"

"What are those little orange flags for, daddy?"

Jacob pointed at the hearse. There was a small flag above the passenger door that read FUNERAL and then he pointed at the other cars in the motorcade, which all had the same bright orange flags above the passenger door.

Daddy closed his eyes for a moment and Jacob noticed a tear stream down his cheek. "They're to let everyone on the roads know that there is a funeral, Jacob. They are there so the other cars on the road let the line of cars by."

"Do we have one of those flags on our car?"

Daddy nodded. "Yes, we do."

The memories of his grandmother's funeral were burned into his tiny, inquisitive, three year old mind. Throughout his childhood and into his teenage years, years after his grandmother had been buried, he could still remember the February day. In his mind, he could still look down, remember the blue winter boots that he wore, the tiny black suit and red bow-tie; and even remembered slipping on the cracked ice while walking into the vestibule into which his grandmother's coffin was being wheeled.

He could still remember watching in wonder as the funeral director (back then, he just saw a man in a suit), as he opened the casket lid, gently unfolded the satin linings, draped it over the outer sides of the casket, and straightened his grandmother's dress. He watched as the man pulled a shiny, silver looking crank from under the head of the casket and turned it. Jacob watched as gramma seemed to rise up and become more visible.

The image of gramma lying there was a memory he would never forget. The first image of death in his life; just a toddler of three when she had passed, and with his parents seemingly inconsolable, he was there to experience it on his own.

There was a slight smile on her face.

But not too much.

He remembered overhearing the phone conversations his mother had. "Don't make her look like she's laughing, that would be strange. But we certainly don't want a frown. Just make her look like she's sleeping. At least as best you can."

When Jacob was standing on the riser, his small hands gripping the satin, he looked at his grandmother. *Where did you go, gramma?*

Just a week ago, he had been sitting on her lap in the kitchen. She was peeling a banana, getting ready to do the choo-choo. She'd held him in one big, meaty arm, as she laid the half peeled banana on the table. She looked over at Jacob, and smiled her warm, grandmotherly smile as she started to tug down on the peel with one hand. "Get ready for the choo-*choo!*"

Jacob squealed and clapped his hands, throwing his head back in laughter. "*Hoo-weee!*" She picked up the banana and hovered it in front of his mouth. She smiled and moved it around in a circle. "Here comes the train! Here comes the choo-*choo!*"

Not even seventy-two hours later, she had a massive heart attack. He remembered the midnight phone call, his mother and father sobbing in each other's arms as he stood in the hallway, holding his blankie, the faint light from the bedside lamp spilling out into the darkness. He remembered his father coming into his bedroom not much later, turning on the light, telling him to get dressed.

He dragged blankie at his side, wandering into mommy and daddy's room. Mommy was sniffling. There was an open suitcase on the bed, and she was placing folded clothes inside. "What's wrong mommy?"

She looked over at him and held her arms out. He ran to her and hugged her waist. "Oh, Jacob. Gramma went to Heaven tonight, honey. And we have to go help her get there."

He dropped his blankie on the floor and looked up at mommy. "How do we help her?"

She closed her eyes and covered her mouth with her hand.

After a few minutes, she opened her eyes and bent down, closer to Jacob.

"Well," she said. She put her arms around him, as her voice was quiet against the pelt of the rain against the windowpanes. He could hear daddy walking downstairs as the garage door opened. "We will pray for her," she said. "And then we will say goodbye to her. Because she is going to Heaven."

Mommy's voice quivered and Jacob hugged her tight.

"Why are you crying, mommy? Can't we go with her?"

She sniffled and reached up to wipe her cheeks. "No, honey. She is going on her own. It's something we all do one day."

"When will she come back?"

She sniffled and covered her face with her free hand. "She isn't coming back, honey."

And that was the first time that Jacob had remembered crying over the death of his Grandmother.

At that tender age, he still did not understand why she was not returning after her trip to Heaven. And when he was nearly thirty, he could still remember the conversation with his mother in the bedroom, and later pounding his fists on the carpet as hot tears streamed down his red flushed cheeks.

And then, a few days after his temper tantrum, Jacob had been standing on the riser, leaning over the casket, reaching forward, about to touch her cold, firm cheek.

His mother was standing above him, and he could hear her sniffles.

He looked at his grandmother, and the slight smile on her face. "She looks so peaceful," he overheard her mother say through the sniffles. "They did such a good job. It's like she's just sleeping."

And Jacob turned and watched his mother, talking with his aunt next to him. He could see that the dark lines went down her cheeks. Smudges under her eyes. And then when he turned back to look at his grandmother, lying below them in the coffin, he reached his finger out again…slowly…closer to his grandmother's cheek, as he leaned over the side of the casket.

"Jacob!" His mother grabbed his arms and pulled him back. "What are you doing!?"

"I…" he said. His eyes were wide and his mouth quivered. He saw mommy. There was a scowl on her face. Her mouth was hanging open. "Jacob! Don't do that!"

"I just wanted to see if she would wake up and do the choo-*choo*…" Jacob frowned and buried his face into his mother's skirt. She reached her arm down and rubbed his back. "I'm sorry, honey. She's not going to do the choo-choo with you anymore. She's gone to Heaven, hon."

Twenty-seven years after they buried his grandmother, Jacob sat on the steps of the University library. He wore blue jeans and his trademark long sleeve white shirt despite an oppressively hot afternoon, and he continually wiped his brow with the side of his arm. His red tie hung down low between his legs, and swayed in a passing breeze. His messy, parted, brown hair hung low and concealed the sides of his cheekbones. A vintage Nikon hung around his neck, and he fished for a pack of Salem cigarettes from his breast pocket. He drew a cigarette out, clamped on it between his teeth, and looked up.

His thesis research partners, Darryl Coleman and Susan Baroni, were approaching him.

He knew they would want to share the project. He'd known them for years, all from the same street in the same town, with the same aspirations. They each chose University for their undergraduate, and all got accepted for the same MFA program: Paranormal Studies.

Jacob had been enthralled with the supernatural and paranormal since he had been a small child, and Susan owned a Parker Brothers Ouija board, so they became fast friends. Darryl lived just three houses down from Jacob, and came from the only black family on their street.

Neither Jacob nor Darryl had been athletic, and the day that Jacob first met Darryl, was when the group of neighborhood kids was playing dodge ball on the cul-de-sac. It was a daily after school game, and Jacob used to sit on the sidelines.

But he had remembered the day from when they were young boys vividly. As the other boys and girls were shouting and hurling the inflatable ball at one another, Jacob had been sitting with his knees drawn up to his chest; his arms wrapped around his legs, his right arm reaching down and digging in the dirt with a small rock.

After a minute, he noticed a shadow.

Someone was blocking the sun. He stopped digging with his rock and looked up.

"You're blocking my light," Jacob said, looking up. He saw a silhouette surrounding by bright sunlight.

The new boy moved to the side and Jacob dropped his rock, holding his arms up and shielding eyes. "Jeez that's bright!"

"Sorry."

Jacob rose to his feet and wiped his hands on his jean cutoffs. He ignored the dirt on his behind. "You're the new kid, right?"

The new boy slowly nodded.

"I'm Jacob," he said, extending his hand out to the new boy. "We all pretty much hang out together. What's your name?"

"Darryl," he said. The young boy looked over at the other children as a large, red inflatable ball bounced across the pavement.

The group of kids scattered and squealed, as if the ball were on fire. Girls shrieked and boys gave each other high-fives as they had evaded the attack of the ball. One small red-headed boy yelped when the ball smacked against his shin, and the other children chanted "It's your turn! It's your turn!" The small boy adjusted his glasses and picked up the ball, carrying it to the other side of the pavement.

Jacob looked over at Darryl and raised his chin as he spoke. "You just moved in, right?"

Darryl nodded.

Jacob gestured over to the other kids, as the teams gathered again at the opposite end of the pavement, huddling together in a group.

The kids watched the small red-headed boy place the ball on the ground, just in front of his feet. He took a few steps back and kicked the ball across the pavement towards the huddled children.

The girls shrieked once again as they repeated the process.

Jacob nodded at Darryl. "They're short one."

He shook his head. "Can't. I have asthma," he said. "Bad too. Doc says I can't run."

Jacob put his hands on his hips. "Well then," he said. "You play cars? I have a huge city I'm building in my back yard. Digging through the dirt, everything. You wanna see it?"

Darryl's eyes widened.

He smiled and nodded, as the two boys dashed across the street, through the trees towards Jacob's sand city in the backyard.

Over the years, the two boys bonded and he and Darryl used to build underground forts in the back behind Jacob's house after school.

Jacob's other research partner, Susan Baroni, had moved to the block just as Jacob and Darryl were heading to Freshman year. The same age as he and Darryl, Susan's family had moved from Summerside. When her family had first moved to the block, Darryl leaned closer to Jacob as they watched the large semi pull up towards the house across the street.

A small framed man with a receding hairline and a bushy mustache emerged from the front door and started pointing and speaking with the movers. The man's voice carried across the street as the two boys huddled in the trees.

The man was speaking rapidly but neither Jacob nor Darryl could understand what the man was saying. The man then headed towards the street down the driveway and over a few steps towards the small, front strip of grass, and grasped the small wooden real estate sign, which Jacob noted had been there for months. The man reached up to the top strip of wood and grasped the SOLD sign, rocking it back and forth.

"That guy looks familiar," Darryl said. "Like we've seen him before."

Jacob turned his head slowly and looked at Darryl, as the man pushed the post sideways.

"What do you mean?" Jacob asked.

"They were on the news a while back," Darryl said, not moving his head, intently focused on the man. They watched as he grasped the wooded sign, rocking the post in circles. Darryl turned and looked at Jacob, who turned his head and they made eye contact. "That's them," Darryl said, moving closer to Jacob and lowering his voice to a whisper.

Darryl scowled as Jacob spoke a little too loudly. "Them *who*?"

Darryl looked back across the street and shook his head. Jacob returned his attention to the man as well. He'd gotten the post out of the ground and hoisted it under his arm.

He headed up the driveway and back towards the house, holding the sign in his opposite hand. If the man heard his outburst, he wasn't showing any signs that he had.

Darryl placed his hand on Jacob's shoulder, and Jacob turned and looked at his friend in the eyes.

"They were on the news a while back," Darryl said. "Bunch of guys who think Hitler is still alive painted their house with swastikas."

Jacob gasped and looked back across at the house, as the man retreated into the garage on the side of the house. "I think I remember that!"

Darryl nodded. "House was torched. Big trial after." He then turned and looked at Jacob.

"Did you see it?" Darryl asked. "They had the trial on the news."

Jacob shook his head. "How can that stuff even go on in the world?"

Darryl shrugged his shoulders. "Believe me, it does."

Jacob shook his head slowly as a young teenage girl walked down the driveway. She flipped one side of her hair behind her shoulders and picked up a small, rolled newspaper at the end of the driveway. She paused and looked across the street, directly where he and Darryl had been hiding in the bushes.

She stood for a few minutes, watching them watching her, but she did not say anything. She opened her palm and shielded her eyes from the sun, and he and Darryl retreated further into the bushes.

"Do you think she sees us?" Jacob asked.

Their vision was shielded by branches and small, bright green leaves. Darryl moved back deeper into the shrubbery. "I think she did."

But she said nothing, did not approach, and simply turned and walked back up the driveway, her small skirt shuffling back and forth with each step.

There was a Funeral Home not far from their school. Not far from it, on the same road, was a small cemetery, surrounded by a stone wall with wrought iron spires. Jacob sat in his room, and stared at the mirror.

His mother had called his brown hair a mop, but it suited him.

And as he stared at his reflection, he knew that there was something about that cemetery. He pulled open his desk drawer and fished out a yellowed newspaper article.

Local Cemetery Rumored to be Haunted

The small photo that accompanied the blocks of text was crude and looked older than it was, but the stone wall and spires were unmistakable: it was the edge of Resurrection Cemetery.

Although the piece was featured in the Arts and Entertainment section, Jacob was fascinated with it. He gasped when he saw it, his mouth dropped open, and he ran, newspaper in hand, to his father's study.

He fished a pair of scissors from the cup of pens and pencils near the large, leather blotter, and clipped the article. He chewed on his lower lip as his eyes moved from left to right, as he held the small piece of paper.

That was it.

He picked up the phone and punched Darryl's number in.

After several rings, he recognized his friend's voice. It took several minutes to convince him, but Darryl finally agreed to go to Resurrection. Within minutes, the doorbell chimed and they headed to the garage.

"You have some weird death fascination," Darryl said as they piled into Jacob's mother's small Honda sedan.

Darryl looked over at Jacob as he placed the key into the ignition. "Uh…" Darryl said. "Your mom gave you permission to take the car?"

Jacob looked over at Darryl and cracked a smile. "She's in Philly," he said. "Her niece is getting married."

"Your dad?"

Jacob shrugged. "At the hospital. Some big surgery they're doing today. Doubt he'll be back anytime soon."

Darryl scoffed and shook his head. "But you just have your permit!"

Jacob threw the car into reverse and looked behind his shoulder as he navigated the lengthy driveway. "So do you!"

Darryl leaned his head against the window and placed his head in his open palms. "But you know two permits don't equal a license!"

Jacob shook his head and charged down the street. Jacob drove the car as if he had years of experience, and handed Darryl the article. "This is why we're going," Jacob said.

Darryl picked up the small, yellowed piece of paper. The car grew quiet as he started reading it, and Jacob fumbled with the radio.

"This is all a bunch of mumbo jumbo," he said. "It's written by a Ghost Tour company."

"And that's Resurrection Cemetery they're talking about," Jacob offered.

Darryl looked out the window as the sun sank beneath the horizon. He shook his head. "And you chose to go in the dark."

"Absolutely. The spirits are more active then."

"Why would you want to contact spirits anyway?"

Jacob thought of the funeral.

And when he had touched Gramma's cheek. It was the only funeral that he had attended in his life up to that point. He remembered that several years prior, an Uncle had passed away that he hadn't spent much time with him, and hadn't really known him all that well, so he stayed home when his parents left town to attend the funeral. But other than that, his only direct experience with death had been back when he was only three years old. "Death is the biggest mystery of life," he said. "And I want to discover what happens."

"And so going to a cemetery at night that some Ghost Tour company says is haunted is going to answer that question for you?"

They approached the side of Resurrection Cemetery and Jacob pulled the car next to the crumbling, cracked sidewalk. He cut the ignition and looked over at Darryl. "Don't know," he said. And then he looked ahead and pointed. "But look there."

Darryl gasped. "Waxley?!"

Jacob looked back at Darryl and nodded. "You bet."

He opened his door and stepped out, as Darryl followed at a much more careful pace. Jacob headed over towards the stone wall and pulled himself upwards, struggling to see over the top of the wall. "Hey! Darryl! Give me a boost, will ya?"

Darryl moved behind Jacob, stooped down, linked his fingers together, and held his hands out in a bowl beneath Jacob's feet. "Step up," he said. Jacob stepped in Darryl's cupped hands and hoisted himself above the top edge of the wall. He gasped.

"What is it?" Darryl asked.

Jacob looked out into the cemetery. Mounds of dirt surrounded the monuments in the early evening darkness. "So they were right!"

He could tell Darryl was starting to struggle from holding his weight.

Jacob looked out at the sea of markers and tried to steady himself on Darryl's shoulders. Darryl grunted. "Who's right?"

Jacob looked down and nodded as Darryl assisted Jacob down to the ground. "The tour people," Jacob said. "All the graves are dug up."

Jacob could tell that Darryl's face had shifted, but it was dark against the infancy of the night. He saw his head cock to the side. Jacob jumped from Darryl's hands and steadied himself. He headed towards the opening in the gate at the end of the deserted street.

After a few steps, he turned around, and saw Darryl standing beside the car. "Are you coming?"

Darryl took a few steps forward, amidst turning his head in the direction of the cemetery. "What did you see in there, Jacob?"

Jacob turned and headed to the opening. He answered without looking back. "Just what I thought I would. Mounds of dirt everywhere. I'd be willing to bet there are no bodies in there."

He heard Darryl's sneakers slide to a stop on some gravel on the pavement. Jacob turned around and saw Darryl standing a few feet behind him. "So what does this have to do with exploring death?"

Jacob shrugged his shoulders. "I don't know…yet. But I want to find out. I'd heard rumors about this cemetery. That's the first time I actually *saw* it!"

"And what are you trying to do by going in there?"

Jacob gave an exasperated sigh. "Look. Are you coming with me or not?"

Darryl approached Jacob. "Yeah, yeah. I'm coming!"

And the two boys walked next to each other, in the darkness, against the stone wall which surrounded Resurrection, to the large, rusted iron gates.

Jacob looked beyond the gates.

There was a large swath of thick, mature oak trees, shielding the road from what lay ahead. He squinted but it didn't help. For he knew what lay ahead.

He'd heard about Waxley for years.

Some of the other kids on the street had talked about it. A few claimed to have visited the old, abandoned mortuary. They even said that they found old caskets. And urns filled with ashes.

But that evening, as he and Darryl crunched through the leaves and fallen twigs, the destination wasn't the old building of the Waxley Mortuary. What interested Jacob that evening was the adjoining cemetery.

"All the graves were dug up," he said, looking over at Darryl as they navigated the overgrowth of the dark forest. They seemed to get deeper, and the night moon, now present, offered little light.

"Dug up?" Darryl asked. "All of them? Why?"

Jacob fished a flashlight from his backpack and flipped it on. A circle of light highlighted dead leaves and overgrown branches. "No one knows," he said. Jacob aimed the flashlight to their right. "I think it's over that way."

The two boys headed in that direction, through more dead bushes and giant trees. "I think it's not far now," Jacob said, shining the flashlight ahead. The light was reflected back by dead branches with browned leaves, and didn't reach very far ahead.

As they headed forward, reaching through the branches, they came to a clearing.

"I think this is the edge of the cemetery," Jacob said, shining his flashlight around the area. Through a layer of overgrown shrubs, he saw the edges of an iron fence. "I don't think they continued the stone wall all the way around," he said. "I think I see an iron fence through those bushes."

Darryl moved up beside Jacob and looked ahead. Jacob saw Darryl point ahead in the darkness. "Just there? And then we'll be out of these trees?"

"I think so."

The boys foraged ahead.

Jacob kept his arm extended, pushing the thick, dead brush apart.

They eased themselves through thick brush that reached up towards their shoulders, and stopped at the iron fence. As they looked ahead, they stood in silence.

There they were.

The sea of gravestones was highlighted by the infant moonlight, bathed in blue on the stone tops and rising through the darkness of the untended grass like lonely lights in a deep, uninspired, unexplored ocean.

As Jacob shined the flashlight into the cemetery clearing, Darryl scaled the fence and landed heavy on his feet next to a mound of dirt.

Jacob shook his head. "Will you wait a minute? I want to make sure there's another entrance somewhere along here."

Darryl chuckled. "You mean to say you've had a change of heart? Are you scared now?"

Jacob scoffed as he moved along the edge of the fence. "No, but I want to see if there is another entrance so we don't have to keep hopping over fences."

Jacob approached an opening further down and walked through. Once inside the cemetery, he turned and shined his flashlight back into the woods. The light didn't reach far, but he thought he saw the edge of a building. "I think this is the path they used to take when they buried people."

He heard Darryl's footsteps approach and shined his flashlight on the ground.

The edge of the grass was just under where Darryl stopped and stood, and as Jacob moved the flashlight to his right; he saw dirt and rocks, for about ten to twelve feet, before the overgrowth of the grass took over again.

"This is where the hearses would drive through from the Mortuary," Jacob said.

Darryl took a few steps closer to the woods. "It's all overgrown…"

As the two boys turned around towards the cemetery clearing, Jacob held his arm out and stopped Darryl from moving forward. "Wait," he said.

He shined the flashlight deeper into the cemetery. The road wound around towards the right, and there were monuments in various states of disrepair; a mound of dirt surrounded each one.

"I think I saw something," Jacob said.

Darryl scoffed. "Would you stop it? This isn't the time to play games."

"Shhh!" Jacob hissed. He lowered his voice and stood right next to Darryl. "I'm not playing games!"

Jacob could feel his heart beating in his chest.

He shined he flashlight deeper into the cemetery, as the clouds parted above them and the moonlight filtered down.

Monuments rose from the ground, some tipping into the earth at an angle.

He squinted his eyes.

Movement in the shadows ahead. He froze. "Be still," he whispered. He could hear Darryl's breathing just next to him, and his heart beat fast inside his chest. "I saw something move in the shadows."

A mist covered the ground in a swirling layer. He heard Darryl gasp. "I saw!" he whispered.

Jacob felt his heart pound.

He scanned the area.

There was movement in the shadows, far across from where they stood. He saw the glimpse of a shadow, movement that appeared like someone walking. Long, flowing hair. And they froze when they saw what looked like a woman.

The mist concealed her lower half as the air cooled, the darkness shrouded her identity.

Who was she?

Only their tiny, short breaths could be heard against the silence of the night. As Jacob watched the woman walk between the monuments at the far edge of the cemetery, towards the trees, thoughts raced through his mind.

Questions about who...or what...the woman could be.

She now appeared bathed in light; glowing; the mist that swirled in the graveyard becoming a veil of secrecy; enhancing the mystery.

She turned and approached.

Jacob grabbed Darryl's arm and they spilled backwards.

He helped Darryl back up to his feet and they charged towards the woods.

They tore through the brush, deeper into the trees, as the dead branches scraped against their arms.

And as the old building came into sight, Jacob could feel a sense of relief wash over him; he saw the broken windows and crumbling brick and stone; he dared not look back towards the cemetery.

He could feel the grip of the cemetery behind them; thoughts which pierced their minds and chilled their backs:

Come hither…

"Get back to the gates!" Jacob hissed.

A light emanated from within the forest as branches cracked.

He pushed Darryl's back as they stumbled through the dead, rotting shrubbery, further and away, down the stone path, and out towards the street.

His mother's small Honda was just ahead.

They ran and spilled against the sides of the car, struggling to catch their breath. Jacob dug into his pocket and fumbled with the keys, his hands shaking as he attempted to find the lock.

He peered over the roof of the car.

Come deep within...

He flung the door open and dove inside the car. Darryl got inside just as fast. They slammed their doors, as Darryl sat in the front seat, his breathing heavy and labored. Jacob leaned back in the driver's seat and closed his eyes, concentrating on the pounding in his chest. He focused on each breath, shoving the keys into the ignition, and the engine roared to life.

He shouted out as he turned his head and opened his eyes.

A woman stood just outside the driver's side window – and Jacob screamed. Darryl's face shifted, his eyes wide, yelling in unison with Jacob.

She stood, outside the door, a blurred, undescriptive image through the fogged glass. She cocked her head to the side, unassuming, until she reached her hand out…slowly…closer towards the car window. She extended her finger, slowly. Jacob's eyes widened as her finger closed in on the glass, getting closer…creeping closer…to the edge of the glass.

And then she tapped slowly.

And the woman raised her arm, waving.

Jacob reached over and lowered the window. And it was no woman at all. It was the girl from across the street.

His mouth dropped open and he felt Darryl leaning over the console, shoulder to shoulder.

She smiled. "Um…hello?"

Jacob's eyes widened. It was her. He recognized her long hair. But it looked wet. A bit dirty. She stood next to the car shivering. "Don't you guys live on the same street as me?"

Jacob looked over at Darryl. He had an equally perplexed look on his face. Jacob opened his mouth, but it was Darryl who spoke first: "What are you doing out here?"

She let out a nervous laugh. "It's kind of silly, really."

Darryl's eyes narrowed, as he sat back in the passenger seat. Jacob looked over at him, and then back at the girl.

Jacob's eyes followed her hands as she placed them on the edge of the window. She looked down as her face fell. "Honestly… I think you might find me a little strange."

Jacob's face shifted. "What do you mean?"

She raised her eyes and looked directly at each of the boys. "Well…we just moved here, as you know, and I haven't really met anyone from the area yet."

"We've seen you at school," Darryl said.

She nodded. "I'm Susan. And yes, I've been around school, but I have basically been invisible. I haven't really had any human interaction. But that's beside the point."

"Go on…" Jacob said.

"Anyway," she said. "I'm a writer. And I come here…to the cemetery…and write in my journal."

Jacob knew that she had kept to herself. A quiet loner. But didn't know that she even knew about the stories behind Waxley and Resurrection, with her being from another area. "Do you need a ride home?"

Her face brightened as she nodded and reached out towards the back door handle. He felt Darryl's hand squeezing his forearm, but he ignored it.

As she got inside the backseat, the two boys turned and looked at her. In the interior light of the small Honda, it was apparent that she was dirtier than they had first realized. Her hair was caked in dirt.

Darryl looked at Jacob as he threw the car into gear and drove away. As he turned the car around, he got a glimpse of the cemetery through a break in the stone wall, as his mind was penetrated once again.

The best thinking time is spent inside the coffin…

He shivered for a moment, looking down at the steering wheel. He sat, the car running, stuck in the middle of a 'k' turn, until Darryl nudged his arm. "Hey! You okay?"

He looked back at Susan in the rearview mirror.

She was smoothing her hair with her hands. She looked up, and made eye contact with him, as he felt chills run through his spine.

We all wind up there.

STAINED
GLASS

IN THE FOLLOWING YEARS after the incident in Resurrection Cemetery, Jacob and Darryl grew closer to Susan. Her mysterious aura had lifted over time, and Jacob and Darryl had forgotten about the mystery surrounding her presence in the cemetery, the cakes of dirt in her hair, and the muss of her clothing.

The car ride home from Resurrection had initially been awkward. As she sat in the back seat in silence, Darryl had fiddled with the radio. After a few minutes, and as the car had pulled up on their shared street, where each of their houses sat just yards from one another, Jacob had broken the ice and discovered her purpose for being there, by asking Susan why she had been at the cemetery. They discovered that they had a shared interest in the macabre. And upon discovering that, Jacob's eyes had widened, and a new friendship was born.

It hadn't been much longer when he learned that Susan owned a Parker Brothers Ouija board, and despite strict Judaism in her family, she had an interest in séances, as well as assuming herself to be clairvoyant.

Jacob remembered in the following years, when they sat in her basement, just the three of them sitting on the cold, hard cement surrounding a single burning candle, in an attempt to contact Jacob's grandmother, Susan's mother, and Darryl's cousin.

But the teenage séances did not yield contact, as far as they knew. When they gasped as the candles in the middle of their circle flickered as they chanted and requested spirits to speak with them, Darryl insisted it was simply air movement. Even though Susan retorted and insisted the flickering candle was a sign. That the spirits *were* communicating with them, that the method may not always be in the form he might be used to.

In the years that followed, and as the bond between them strengthened, they chose to apply to the same University, and lucky for them, all were accepted. While they had different majors during their undergraduate work, they decided as a trio to explore Paranormal Studies for the Master's Degree. Darryl took the most convincing, but he expressed an interest in Theology in his Undergrad, so he opted for the unorthodox choice of study for his Post-Graduate work.

Jacob called Darryl early on the morning they were scheduled to meet to start research. Jacob asked Darryl to call Susan so they could all meet and head over to the mortuary that evening at sunset. They both knew that Jacob had wanted to explore the mortuary as part of the thesis.

"It's a little hot for that shirt, isn't it bro?" Jacob recognized Darryl's deep, baritone voice.

Jacob looked up and raised his arms over his eyes. "It's light. It breathes."

The sun was shining right behind Darryl, and all Jacob saw was a dark silhouette, despite raising his hands to cover his eyes from the brilliance of the sun. He could tell by the outward curvature of his cheeks that Darryl had a smirk on his face. Darryl leaned in closer and Jacob saw his eyebrows were raised. "That tie is too long for you. I've been telling you that."

"You know I *always* wear the red one on Tuesdays," Jacob said, rolling his eyes. "And I've been telling you *that*."

He placed the camera on the cement, unbuttoned his sleeves, and pushed them up to his elbows. "I didn't know it was going to be this hot today."

Jacob stood up and placed the camera back around his neck. It swung a bit. Darryl's eyes widened and he reached out to steady it. "Yo, *dude*! You know how much that's worth, right?"

Jacob nodded but said nothing.

"My Uncle said we could use it for the project, but not trash it! He's had that for years. A lot longer than we've known each other."

Jacob shrugged his shoulders as he and Darryl looked over at Susan, who stood, clasping her arms across her breasts. A light breeze caught her hair. He placed his hand on her shoulder, and she looked up at him. He looked into her eyes. "Do you still have the Ouija?"

She looked down, closed her eyes and nodded.

"I had to rummage through my closet. But I found it. But in all honesty…this has been at the bottom of my closet for years. I'm not really sure I want to go back to it. Are you sure we should be using this in a mortuary?"

Jacob stood back and clasped his hands together. "We're going to need it if we're going to try and contact him."

Susan looked up slowly. There were bags under her eyes. "Him?"

Darryl looked directly at Jacob, over at Susan, then back and locked eyes with Jacob. "I think the exploration part is fascinating. And the research. But I'm not so sure about attempting to contact the dead."

"I'm not planning on contacting the dead in *general*, I just want to specifically speak with Ned McCracken. He's the one who disappeared from Waxley. Could you imagine an interview with a spirit for our project? Talk about publication!"

Susan shifted her backpack on her shoulders. "We don't know that he's dead though," she said. "We just know —"

"— that he disappeared," Jacob said. "Yes, I know. I've read the investigations. I know the rumors too. But you honestly think he's still alive after all this time? That happened decades ago. Before even our *parents* were born."

Darryl shrugged his shoulders. "Stranger things have happened. But he's most likely dead."

Jacob bent down and grabbed his own backpack. "So you both are in?"

Darryl and Susan looked at each other.

"If we get published we gain notoriety," Jacob said. "Think of what we leave as a legacy. None of us have kids. We're not celebrities. We just have our work. And this is it. We need to break new ground, guys."

Darryl looked over at Susan. He raised his eyebrows as she looked over at him. She looked away, closed her eyes and nodded. Darryl looked back at Jacob and nodded as well.

"Then it's settled then," Jacob said. The three of them started down the steps and across the main lawn, opting for a route under the pink blooming cherry trees. "So this is the deal," Jacob said. Susan fished some black licorice whips from her bag and offered some to the guys.

"We'll go at dusk today," Jacob continued, in between bites of his licorice whip. "I'll have the equipment in my truck."

Darryl looked over at Jacob. "Do you think we should start with the equipment yet? Don't you think we should wait until we've declared our thesis statement? At least then the University will assist with getting us access from the city."

Susan handed Jacob another whip. "Darryl's right, Jacob. We can't just explore an abandoned building like that without permission from the city."

Jacob scoffed. "I need to get over there," he said. "I have to look around. I've been researching this guy for months now. Watching videos of the place. I have to see it in person. And *experience* it. Just think of this as a little 'pre-research' research."

Susan nodded. "Yes…but we have to stay within the parameters of the law. And I'm not going to bring the Ouija tonight. Tonight you're on your own. We can just look around, that's it."

Jacob's looked over at Susan with wide eyes, his mouth open, as he lowered the licorice whip slowly. "What do you mean you're not going to bring it?"

She sighed. "Look, Jay. We haven't even been in there yet. Let's just look around. No equipment yet. No Ouija boards. Let's look and see what we're dealing with before going in full force."

Jacob shrugged. "Look, either you guys are with me or not. But I want this to be the thesis they *publish*. I already have a ton of book and microfiche research. I've got old photos. Yellowed newspaper clippings. I just need to see some of this in person."

"By breaking and entering?" Darryl asked.

Jacob tossed the remainder of his whip in some nearby hedges and turned around as the group stopped walking. "No, man! Have you seen that place? There's no *breaking* at all! The place is falling apart and we can just stroll right in. I just want to poke around a bit. We're not going to *take* anything!"

And then they each looked up as they heard the crunch of footsteps in the gravel approaching them. The man who was heading towards them was dressed in a t-shirt and tattered jeans – rather unorthodox for a University professor. He looked more like a student. But that's what the three of them liked about Professor Howell. He was smiling and adjusted his glasses. "And how are my three favorite graduate students doing this afternoon?"

Jacob turned to face Professor Howell and spoke first. "We are discussing the project," he said.

Professor Howell's eyes lit up. He hooked his hair around his ear and crossed his arms. "Go on," he said.

"Jacob wants to visit Waxley tonight," Susan said.

Professor Howell's mouth dropped open as he listened. He then unhooked his arms and raised his index finger. "No, Jacob, no. You can't visit that property until you have officially delivered your thesis statement in class. And even then, you have to wait until the University gets permission from the city for you to explore the premises. There are certain avenues you must adhere to for this research, Jacob. You have to have your sponsorship in place first."

Jacob looked over directly at Professor Howell. "Didn't you research this same subject?"

Professor Howell nodded as Darryl and Susan looked on.

Jacob folded his arms. "I read your thesis."

Professor Howell chuckled, and took a step back. Jacob noted that his teeth were exceptionally white and straight. His arms dropped to his sides as he shifted from foot to foot. "As you should have!"

Jacob cracked a thin smile, but his arms remained folded. "So you certainly understand why I am doing this, right? Why I am taking this route?"

"Sure. I see a lot of myself in you."

Jacob scoffed and reached around to adjust his backpack. And then looked Professor Howell squarely in the eyes. "Yours was published. I want mine to be too."

Darryl reached over and touched Jacob's arm. "You mean ours."

Jacob shook his head, looked off towards the courtyard and bit his lower lip as Professor Howell picked up his briefcase and headed forward. "Look guys, it's almost time for your next class. Don't let me hear that you went to Waxley tonight."

He walked a few more steps and turned around to face the students. "I'm serious, guys. Since you guys already know that this was my thesis too back when I was a grad. *Don't* let me hear that you went to Waxley tonight. You came to me last semester asking if you could tackle this subject. And I reluctantly said yes. But don't get overeager and overexcited. If you even go, it's going to be supervised by the University. All parts of it. Period."

Jacob waved his arms. "Alright, alright." And then he watched Professor Howell head back towards the library. After he rounded the corner, Jacob looked back at Susan and Darryl, who stood looking back at him.

"I'm going to go," he said. "You guys can either come, or not. But I've watched enough footage of this place. I want to see it in person. I'm going to go at sunset. You guys can either come with me or not, I won't hold it against you if you don't. But I'm going, with or without you."

Later that afternoon, Jacob set the Nikon on the small, wooden desk on the side wall of his off-campus apartment bedroom. The blinds were drawn, and it was cool and dark. He flicked on his small, steel desk lamp, and flopped in the chair. It was much quieter than usual.

There wasn't the calling of classmates in the exterior hallways, the hooting and hollering had always interrupted his research in previous weeks. Now he could focus with peace and quiet in his solitude.

The University was at the genesis of a short fall break, and his roommate was back in California visiting his family for the week. He powered up his desktop computer, and after a few minutes of booting up, he navigated to the file on his desktop marked THESIS, clicking on it. He double clicked on the file marked ARTICLE, and a dated and cracked copy of an old newspaper article filled the screen:

Local Mortician Gone Missing

"Police have officially declared local mortician Ned McCracken a missing person after the mysterious disappearances of the staff at the Waxley Mortuary at the end of Ascension Avenue. The Mortuary has been attached to Resurrection Cemetery on the south side of town for decades, until Mr. Waxley's sudden death of a stroke. Upon his death, the Waxley Mortuary and Funeral Home was left to Mr. McCracken to own and operate. Police and rescue personnel were called to the mortuary last week, but McCracken has not been able to be located, despite several attempts. The Funeral Home has been sitting abandoned and is swiftly heading to a state of disrepair."

Jacob sat back, took a deep breath and exhaled. He rubbed his eyes with his fingers.

This was too interesting to not start with now.

This was what he was born to do.

And when he stared at the article, he fished through his desk drawer, the large drawer on the bottom where he'd kept all of his gathered research. He pulled out a small, manila folder and fished the photo out.

It was of a man, standing in front of the Mortuary building. It had to have been at least as old as his grandparents.

It was the Mortician, to be certain.

From his research, Jacob had discovered that the man's name was Ned McCracken, and that he had relocated to Miami from the North, worked at Waxley for a period of time, and quite suddenly inherited the operation as his own. And then not long after that, disappeared, seemingly into thin air.

But the photo, he thought, was extraordinary.

It was a large, 8x10 black and white print. It was faded, yellowed, but discernable. He flipped the photo over. There was a water stain on the back, and written in faded black ink: 1938.

It was a fairly close up photo; the man in a dark suit and slicked black, or possibly dark brown hair. Standing in some black and white gardens, with shrubbery and the brick building behind him.

Thoughts flooded his mind of the last time he had visited the grounds when he was a curious high school teenager: the overgrowth had been massive back then; dead; and most likely now, that he was over a decade older, he thought it would be far more untended and still dead.

He flipped the photo and noticed the yellowed edges. And reexamined the water damage.

No date marked either.

But the exposure appeared old. Faded and dull. From the past.

And then, as he held the photo close to his eyes, he leaned under the light.

There it was!

The building was behind him.

The big, old brick building. But it didn't look so old back then. It was challenging to determine the time period, but it was many years ago. Perhaps decades.

He lay the photo on the desk.

"Where did you go, Mr. McCracken?"

David Howell was roughly a decade older than Jacob, Darryl and Susan…but he would never disclose that to them. As he had left them in the courtyard, he turned back just before he met the threshold of the library steps. Though they were too far now to hear, he could see Jacob's head movement. He was clearly speaking to them.

He turned and headed up the steps.

As he opened the door and felt the cool blast of air conditioning, he determined that he would have to meet Jacob at Waxley. There was too much of himself in Jacob. He remembered when he conducted his thesis research, a decade previously. He'd done the same thing. David remembered having similar conversations with his Professor – and getting a very familiar sounding warning: don't go to Waxley until the University gives its approval.

But he hadn't listened, just as he expected Jacob to do. So he knew that he would have to meet him there, regardless of whether Darryl and Susan chose to accompany him or not.

For Jacob should not wander the halls of Waxley Mortuary alone.

The photo that lay on Jacob's desk was one of the rare shots of Ned McCracken, the local Mortician who had gotten to be somewhat of a local celebrity as Waxley Mortuary had become the premiere Funeral Parlor of choice in the city when it was in its heyday. In those years,

there had been a transition of how to care for
the dead: houses were still built with "coffin
corners", where the body would be prepared
and placed on display, usually in a front parlor
in the home.

Waxley Mortuary was cutting edge for its time
– and employed every new preservation
technique – be it formaldehyde (which had
replaced the toxic arsenic which have been
used in the previous century) as well as one of
the first operations to handle the entire
procedure post-death, from retrieval of the
deceased all the way to the burial or cremation.

The black and white in the picture failed to
show the scene, but when the photo was taken,
the world had not been simply black…and
white.

It had been filled with vibrant colors…just as
it always has; just as Jacob had always known
the brilliance of color. So the black and white
photo offered a glimpse into the past; like
looking through a veil, towards the days when
the Waxley Mortuary had been thriving.

But the photo did not show that Ned
McCracken's dark suit had not been black, but

rather a deep shade of blue. He had worn a light blue tie, though in the photo it was depicted as grey.

As Ned stood, when the photo had been taken, he was not surrounded by drab, grey, and softly out of focus grass, shrubs and foliage. The mortuary lawn was a vibrant shade of green; well-manicured and tended. The flowerbeds that surrounded the lawn and lined the front brick walls of the Funeral Home were teeming with colorful flowers.

And so the photo was not an accurate depiction of the scene, but the grainy black and white photography was the best technology of the time.

And then the flash sounded –

– Ned covered his eyes with his arm.

"Pat! Why must you insist we take a photo every time a funeral comes through? You know

I despise my photo being taken!" He scowled and reached up, running his hands across his forehead, past his scalp, and smoothed his jet-black hair. He then buttoned his jacket.

Pat slowly lowered the flash box. He was dressed in much simpler clothes than Ned, but still clean and pressed. "Just documenting it sir."

Ned looked onwards as a black Duesenberg pulled forward. He knew it had to be Mrs. Bannister. She had phoned earlier to make the appointment, as her husband had died, quite suddenly.

The car pulled up with an audible squeak of the brakes, and Ned looked down and admired the thick whitewalls. The stark, round headlamps framed the front engine chrome, and he secretly wished he could afford such an elegant car.

He looked up and saw Mrs. Bannister sitting in the shadows of the back seat, in the back cabin, behind a lengthy, amphibian-like engine, square and unassuming, yet uncompromising and long, signifying grand wealth. Ned wondered how such opulence could still exist after the crash. So many were scarcely surviving.

But the Bannisters were clearly unaffected.

The curtains on the window were drawn partially, and her silhouette was pronounced next to the glass.

As Pat folded the wooden tripod and packed the camera back in its crate, Ned stood and watched as the driver emerged from the opposite side of the gleaming Duesenberg. His tailored black tuxedo was as spotless as the finish on the car, and he pulled a stark white handkerchief from his pocket and polished a smudge on the side of the front hood as he headed around the sculpted front, and to the back door. He nodded at Ned as he spun around, his back towards the rear of the car, and opened the door outwards.

Mrs. Bannister reached her arm outwards, wearing a long- sleeved, black and white dress. A lace border circled the wrist, and she was wearing stark white gloves. The driver gently took her hand and assisted her out of the car.

She stood for a moment, and the driver handed her a matching umbrella. Ned could see that she had been crying. Tears had run down her cheeks. The driver handed her a handkerchief and she wiped her face.

"You're young."

Ned cracked a thin smile and nodded. "I am."

She pursed her lips together as she shifted her umbrella to the other shoulder. She craned her neck out, looking at him more closely. "Aren't morticians supposed to be old?"

Ned nodded his head to the side as he extended his arm. Mrs. Bannister took it as Ned spoke. "Not in all cases," he said. "I've been in this business since I was a young boy. I used to help my father. Now, I am here at Waxley, running the operation."

"I thought these Funeral Homes were a new thing."

Ned nodded. "They are, they've been around for a little over a decade." He reached out to place his hand on her arm, and she snapped her head down. He quickly removed it.

"We are recently licensed to take care of all of your funeral needs right here at this location," he said.

She raised her eyes and looked at him. "So that makes you qualified?"

He smiled and nodded. "Yes. I started working in my father's Funeral Home in Michigan roughly a decade ago. I know I am young. But I am well trained. And Waxley hired me because of that. It's a family business for me, and you are family to me. So please, permit me to take care of your husband."

She sighed and extended her hand. "Well then, good afternoon, Ned," she said, taking a few steps towards him.

He nodded as Pat closed the wooden camera tripod and carried it to the front porch. He laid it down and joined the others.

"We offer our condolences," Ned said. Pat nodded and joined Ned's side.

The driver closed the back door and leaned against the side of the car, packing a cigarette. He placed it between his teeth and struck a match, inhaling deeply and exhaling a large cloud of smoke.

Ned looked away from the driver and over at Mrs. Bannister, who was looking back at him.

Ned placed his arm on Mrs. Bannister's back. "And so you don't want to hold the viewing in your own parlor?"

She shook her head. "Well, it has a coffin corner, but no," she said, and looked up at Ned, directly in his eyes. "He was a non-traditional man. And he always was about progress. And I think this is progress." She looked up at the towering building. "A funeral home…and I would like you to handle everything."

"We are one of the first of our kind," Ned said, as the three of them walked towards the front steps. Mrs. Bannister leaned the arm of her umbrella against her shoulder and looked on at Ned, who continued his explanation of their practice, as Pat stood on his other side, his arms clasped behind his back.

"It's a relatively new concept," Ned said. "To have the funeral outside the private home, that is. It's just getting started."

She nodded.

"Yes. It is new. Just recently my Aunt Hattie passed. We had her funeral in our parlor."

"That's been the tradition," Ned said. "We are a new operation for the concept of a 'Funeral Home', but not new to funerals. We've been embalming and preserving for years."

She looked over at him as they ascended the steps. Her heels clamped on the wooden stairs that led to the cement and brick front porch. "I remember my Aunt Hattie's coffin being surrounded by crushed ice."

Ned nodded.

"Yes. That was common in the past. She was not embalmed?"

Her mouth shifted and she cocked her head to the side. She looked up for a moment at the sky, perhaps to search for an answer. "I honestly am not sure, Mr. McCracken."

"Of course, we are here to cater to your wishes. If you would like crushed ice, we can certainly offer that. I do recommend the embalming procedure, though. It preserves the body."

Just before they reached the large, wooden doors, he turned and faced her.

"Embalming is still relatively new when it comes to preservation," he said. "But it's already moved to a much safer chemical. Formaldehyde."

"What was used before?"

"Many of the chemical solutions were arsenic based, especially in the late nineteenth century."

She reached down with her umbrella, turning around. The driver, still leaning on the Deusenberg, sprang into action and dashed across the front grass and up the wooden steps. He took the umbrella from her and folded it together.

She then turned her attention back to Ned. She took a short breath and appeared to steady herself.

"Well then," she said. "Take me in there. Bernard always thought himself to be at the epitome of society. Everything he did…was cutting edge. At least in his mind. So for his last respects, we will do the same here."

Ned nodded as Pat held the door open.

She looked back over at him and raised her eyebrows. "I've been arguing with his mother since he passed," she said. She was shaking her head and rolling her eyes. "It's hard to believe that old bat is still alive. But she is."

Ned offered a thin smile as he took the other door and held it open on the other side for her. "Well, we are all given different amounts of time in this world," he said.

She looked over at him as she crossed the threshold. Her eyes were wide, her lips pursed, and she said nothing more. This was it. His own first customer at Waxley Mortuary. And with little surprise, it was an elite family; those were quite rare in the depression era. But appreciated. And as he ushered her inside, he did. Not long after, they stood in the foyer, listening to faint organ music wafting in from further inside.

But once they got inside, she remained quiet.

She paused, and looked up at the stained glass windows that surrounded the crest of the foyer. She looked down at the fountain in the center, the water babbling softly as the sweet smell of incense filled the air.

The mood fell further.

Ned heard her sigh.

After a few moments, she raised her eyes and looked up at Ned, over at Pat, and back to Ned.

"Show me the coffins."

"This is our casket selection room."

The Mortician reached inwards and opened the doors, swinging them outwards. The woman raised her head, as he turned the lights on. He saw, now as she was under the lights, when she removed her hat, her hair was actually mussed; a dark brown, plastered to one side of her face. It hadn't seemed noticeable outside, when he initially thought she was more put together. Her dress had a noticeable wrinkle running down the back.

How had he missed that outside?

She was too young to be doing this, he thought. Seemingly so inexperienced. But it did not matter what his opinion was. Because he had seen young women come into this funeral home many times before under Waxley's regime.

And Ned knew it wasn't really his place to judge.

Just merely comfort and assist.

Soft, rose-tinted light emanated from behind several caskets which lined the opposite wall. There were three in the direct view from the archway, but there were a number of other caskets displayed in neat, methodical rows deeper into the room. A wall on the opposite side of the sea of coffins displayed several rows of urns on shelves for cremated remains.

The three caskets in front of them were all open, displaying their white satin interiors. Faint organ music played from an unseen room. She took a few cautious steps forward, towards a powder blue casket on the left, reached her hand out and gently touched the side.

She ran her fingers along the edge.

He cleared his throat. "That's Fisk," he said. "A top of the line casket. Sealed from moisture. Made out of steel. Nothing will penetrate it, guaranteed."

She turned and looked at him, her eye shadow running down her cheeks. "Come again?"

He caught himself.

It was too soon to talk about that. The science of it all. He took a breath and held it for a moment, before releasing it slowly. "You'll see it in the literature. But it helps keep the casket from having any moisture intrusion."

She looked back down at the casket and bit her lower lip. She closed her eyes and shook her head. "I don't even understand what that means," she said.

The sweet, smoky smell of incense filled the air.

He stepped aside and folded his arms at his waist. As he looked over at the young woman, her hands clasped at her waist, the flow of tears running down her cheeks, her eyes red rimmed, she took a slow step forward, closer to the powder blue casket, wiped her cheeks with the back of her hands, and paused. He watched her and knew, without equivocation, that she was about to reach her breaking point.

He had seen this scenario so many times before.

And that is why he always waits for this step in the process. Most emotional breakdowns would occur during the casket selection. There was something about that part of the process – selecting a coffin for their deceased loved one would take on a cold, stark reality and hit them in waves.

He looked at her eyes.

He could see the watering return; the tears were billowing out from her eyes, just approaching the rim of the eyelid, but had not broken again yet.

She was trying to hold it in.

She was trying to be strong.

Ned stood and leaned back against the wall, watching her. He had seen this same scene playing before him, when Mr. Waxley had taken the lead, over and over. When Ned had accompanied a widow with Mr. Waxley, observing and learning. And his reaction had always been the same.

Stone cold and somber.

He would always lower his head, close his eyes. Listen to the crying and the sobbing. After a minute, he opened his eyes, turned around, and grabbed a box of tissues. He held them in front of the sobbing woman. "Please. Take one."

She lowered her hands from her face and looked over at the box of tissues. He held it a bit closer to her, gaining her attention by nodding his head. She slowly reached out and took a tissue from the box. She cleared her throat and dabbed her eyes and grabbed another tissue. Ned returned the tissues to the small hidden table as blew her nose.

He swiftly turned back towards the double doors, and reached out to Mrs. Bannister. His gentle touch of his hand on her back guided her back towards the foyer.

"Come," he said. "Let's wait a few minutes."

He guided her to the opposite wall and towards a discreetly placed door behind a large potted palm. He opened it swiftly to a small office. "It opens up into the parlor suite on the other side," he said. "But the planning office has always been a good retreat from the casket room. I know how it can be intense to be in there."

Ned opened the drawer and placed another tissue box on the desk, leaned over and grabbed a small, cylindrical trash can, and got up from the chair smoothly, glided around the desk and held the can out for her. After a few minutes of silence, and as she dabbed her eyes and nose with the tissue, she took a deep breath, closed her eyes, and exhaled.

"I know this is difficult," he said. "The casket selection is probably one of the most difficult parts of the funeral planning process. It brings a sense of reality to everything, I'm afraid."

She opened her eyes and looked up at him as he stood above her, still holding the trash can. Her cheeks were flushed.

He continued. "But it's a necessary step in the process. We can save it for later, if you like."

She looked up at him. Her face appeared to droop with despair. "But…" she said. She took a few slow steps towards the door. Ned watched as she looked across the foyer and saw the caskets line the wall in the display room. She looked back over at him. "I...wasn't ready for this. He wasn't ready."

He saw her mouth quiver as she bit her lip and studied the floor. She closed her eyes. He sat down across from her, and leaned back in his chair. After a few minutes, she returned to her chair, and as the clock ticked in the otherwise silent office, Ned waited patiently as she took a deep breath and exhaled slowly.

She reached up towards the desk and placed the paperwork in her lap, looking down at it.

And as he watched young Mrs. Bannister slowly page through pamphlets with photos of caskets, chapels, gravestones and urns, a flash of the crematoriums in the basement flashed through his mind, just for an instant.

He knew she wouldn't be ready for that option, at least not right now. Not on this visit. But he wanted to let her know about it. Before the body was to be embalmed. Thankfully she wanted an autopsy. After a few more minutes of discussion she opted to leave.

She would return the following day.

After Mrs. Bannister left, Ned stood at the window and looked outwards. He watched as dark clouds rolled across the sky. The winds were picking up, as the treetops started to sway.

He looked up at the small, round stained glass window above the larger picture window.

Daylight was fading.

Just as it had on the Waxley Funeral Home for decades.

He had been in the business a long time.

As he turned and passed a small wood-framed hanging mirror, he looked at himself. He hadn't appeared to have aged. His skin still had a smooth, youthful appearance. Still no traces of grey in his slicked, black hair.

And as he remembered days in the business, with his father, years ago, back in the days when bodies were displayed in parlors and preserved in ice, he thought he resembled his father. But when Ned was just a young boy, the funeral home business was in its infancy; and his father, an astute businessman, built his own operation when times changed.

Ned's father, the man who had introduced him to the business, in the days when the business had just been licensed.

Back when the funeral home that he spent his earlier days bore the family name: McCracken.

As he continued thinking thoughts of his Father, he wondered if he knew that Ned had followed in the same footsteps.

It had been years since they spoke. Ned didn't know if it was Stephen's death that led to their estrangement. Or perhaps just the fact that he was always number two.

After the incident with Stephen, he left Michigan. And hadn't returned since.

Ned closed his eyes.

He felt the warmth of a single tear stream down his cheek.

Come see my dirty walls.

The last thing he wanted to do was go back up there. There was too much time that he felt he was living a solitary life after Stephen passed.

He remembered the night sleeping in the bushes, outside the McCracken Funeral Home, in the chill of the Michigan fall. When he woke, he heard the chatter of unseen voices; none of which could be deciphered, but each that could be heard.

Come see my bloodied mosquitos.

He shook his head, pinching the crest of his nose with his thumb and index finger. The morning grit was still in his eyes. And he remembered those dead, bloodied mosquito carcasses, smeared on the lime green tiles on the walls in the basement of McCracken Funeral Home.

He sighed and headed out of the office, muttering to himself. "I can't go back there."

Ned's cherry brown loafers clapped against the marble floor in the rear hallway as he headed towards the end by the small, exterior receiving door. He reached into his pocket and felt the cool metal, and pulled a brass keyring. It jingled against the silence of the now quiet mortuary. The organist had gone home, and the incense was no longer burning.

Ned looked up and down the hallway.

Towards the right, he could just see the openings to the front foyer. From the skylights above, the sun still shined through, but daylight was fading. The shadow from the giant potted palm in the center had moved. It always moved towards the end of the day.

He returned his attention to the door, as the lock released, he pushed the door open slowly to darkness. He reached over and opened the light switch.

He had to tell Mrs. Bannister about crematory number seven.

She was far too upset to select a casket for her husband. He could see it in her eyes; he could hear it in her voice.

And the Bannisters were a wealthy family.

And they could certainly afford the special treatment.

At this time, Rosa would have left for the day.

Pat might still be there, tucked away, deep in the administrative offices, planning out details of the care contract. But here, in the darkness, staring at a set of rickety wooden stairs leading down to darkness, underneath the yellow glow of an incandescent lightbulb, he was all alone.

Or so it seemed.

For he could see the cement floor below; downwards into the bowels of the operation. To the lowest level, where the coffin elevator would descend to, as its massive cage doors would slide up into the ceiling, and a wooden coffin would be rolled inside to be pushed upstairs towards the viewing rooms.

Each stair creaked as he slowly descended; the dome of light just above reached just a short distance down towards the landing below. The darkness, he knew, was always the mystery of why he worked there.

There was comfort in the darkness.

For the mystery of the unknown, he thought, could be given a veil and forgotten, or placed in denial. For when the lights would glow, he knew that the vision would not be as welcoming as the shield of black solitude.

Those damn green tiles.

They weren't at Waxley, but they had called his name. When Stephen was still alive. When the door was always propped open for ventilation, despite the stifling Michigan summer heat.

He remembered it like it was yesterday.

Back in the years when he was no longer a boy but not yet a man, the awkward years of ill-fitting clothing and a desire to be taken seriously.

He stood in the foyer, looking down at his shoes. He tipped his toes up, examining the shiny leather, noticing the reflection of the windows above.

It was years ago, but still such a penetrating memory.

He hadn't hit his growth spurt yet.

His hair had already darkened, as it had been much lighter when he was a younger boy. His hair would prove to be a defining characteristic throughout his life. But there, standing in the foyer, when he was just getting started, helping father out, he was young and inexperienced, merely helping out with the family business.

The McCracken Funeral Home.

He had always felt somewhat different.

Especially in those days, before the Great Depression was in full force, Father entered a business that seemed depression-immune: the business of death.

"Death is always certain!" he remembered his Father saying to his mother when he brought the bank papers home from closing. "It's how we live our life that matters. The legacy we leave behind."

Ned had looked up from his bowl of Toasty O's. His big eyes raised towards his parents, who were standing over the small ceramic sink near the kitchen window, passing paperwork between each other. Ned could see them speaking, but his mind was cluttered; he heard nothing.

He looked to his left as his older brother Stephen was quickly polishing off a plate of scrambled eggs. He dug the fork into the yellow piles of fluff, the tines nicking the plate with each stroke. After a moment, Stephen looked across the table at Ned. Stephen paused, sat back, looking at Ned, and leaned up on the table. He raised his eyebrows.

"What is it Ned?"

Ned carefully placed his spoon on the edge of his cereal bowl. "Have you been alright lately?"

Stephen tossed his fork on his plate with a clank. He wiped a napkin across his face, never breaking his stare. "Why would you even need to ask?"

Ned could hear the edge in Stephen's voice. It was the stay-out-of-my-business tone that he took from time to time. Ned also knew of the many times where his older brother's voice was warm, friendly and inviting. But this wasn't one of those times.

Ned could feel his chest tighten. "I'm your brother and I love you."

Stephen tossed his napkin on the table, shook his head and rose from his chair. He went over to mother, who was preparing the percolator on the opposite end of the kitchen. She reached behind her back and tightened her apron as Stephen leaned in and kissed her cheek, telling her goodbye.

He then returned to the table and leaned over the chair, leaning close towards Ned. Stephen looked back towards Mother, and then back at Ned. "You're not my mama. No matter how much you want to be. Now stay outta' my *business*. You hear?"

Ned froze as Father entered the kitchen.

Stephen looked up and smiled. "Have a great day, pop!" And then he looked back down at Ned, as he picked up his small, brown satchel. He locked eyes with Ned, and nodded, turned, and headed out the small wooden rear door. The glass rattled in the pane as he closed it.

Ned stared at the door.

Stephen was always leaving.

Always barking some command, then turning, and leaving. He felt his cheeks grow warm, and he let out a short breath. His eyes were watering as he looked over at Mother and Father.

"Will you see that my pants are pressed before the O'Connor viewing tonight?"

Mother nodded and handed Father a cup of coffee. Her heels clicked against the linoleum as she reached out for Stephen's breakfast plate. She raised her eyes, looked at Ned for a brief moment, and smiled, turned and went back across the kitchen to the sink.

The dishes dropped with a clank as Ned sighed. Father approached him, sipping a steaming cup of coffee. "You going to finish your cereal?" Father stood and looked down at Ned, sitting in his chair. Ned wiped his eyes with his sleeve. The small, wooden chair he was sitting in slid across the tile and Ned stood, his face somber and sullen. He closed his eyes and shook his head.

"You're going to be back down soon, Neddie? We have several bodies scheduled to arrive this morning. I need you shortly."

He raised his eyes as he felt a tear stream down his cheek. "Yes, Father. I will be there."

The wooden doors in front of him slid open.

Ned saw his father scurrying around the room, moving plants. He went to the side windows and opened the drapes as sunlight spilled through. And then he went to the casket placed against the far wall, as Ned saw him lean over the coffin, but wasn't sure what he was doing. His mother held a small feather duster, and moved between several credenzas nestled throughout the walls.

Organ music wafted out.

Father turned around, looked across the room, and had wide eyes when he called for Neddie to come. He always had wide eyes when he needed Neddie to assist with some preparation for a viewing.

Ned opened the sliding wooden doors all the way. He felt a blast of cool air against his face as he watched his father. Ned noticed that his father's hair was already greying at the temples. He held the doors partially closed and watched his father in the viewing room while standing in the foyer. Ned stuck his head through the opening the opening as his father turned around again and waved his arm for Ned to come. "Neddie! Come in here! The family is about to arrive and I need you to arrange the chairs in rows." Ned slid the doors wide open and headed towards stacks of wooden chairs that nearly reached the ceiling. His mother stopped using the small feather duster and looked over at his father, who stuck his arm out and gestured for her to come also.

"Help me, both of you, please. We don't have much time."

Ned's mother tossed the duster on the parlor table and dashed back through the doors, joining his father at the casket, assisting with stain placement. Ned looked over and gasped when he saw the casket on the far wall, surrounded by throngs of flower arrangements, mostly white, some pink. His father adjusted standing lamps on either side of the coffin, and flicked the lights on. Rose tinted light bathed the side of the room. Father headed back to the coffin and pointed back to the side wall. "Neddie, chairs!"

Ned looked up. There were wooden chairs stacked in rows, almost to the ceiling lights. Father pointed over to them. "Just grab them and start lining them up facing the casket. We don't have much time. Family will be here in about ten minutes and I need the room to be ready."

Ned ran over to the stacks of chairs and stood on his tippy toes, reaching high above his head and grabbed the two wood legs of the top chair. He gripped them hard with his hands and looked back at father who had been bent over the casket adjusting the man's collar. But neither parent looked back, both focused on the presentation.

Ned found the string and yanked it downwards as the yellowish glow filled the receiving room on the basement level. Waxley was custom built for funerals, as opposed to having an existing home retrofitted.

The ground outside the basement level was excavated and cleared. A driveway was cemented and Ned saw the Cadillac Hearse parked right outside. She was a beauty. A 1937 model that Everett acquired at a steep discount after his convention that year. It had served them well.

But it wasn't what was sitting outside the giant sliding doors that concerned him. For he saw down the receiving hallway, which led towards darkness. There was a single light at the end of the hall. Down towards crematory number seven.

For that light was always on.

Mr. Waxley insisted.

Even when he briefly lived on the top floor of the building.

Ned remembered, when he had first moved to Miami, just after interviewing for his role, when he had briefly lived on the top floor himself.

And Everett Waxley was a light sleeper. Ned could remember that quite well.

Many nights, as Ned had tossed and turned, he would hear the snap of a switch and see a sliver of light fingering its way into his dark bedroom. And then Everett's footsteps, walking out towards the common area. Those were heavy. Always unmistakable.

And then the creak of the stairs, as he heard Everett slowly descending the stairs to the business below.

One night, as the creaks of the stairs were emitting from a lower part of the building, Ned flung the covers to the side and swung his feet to the cold, hardwood floor. For a moment, he was silent.

Another creak.

And then nothing.

Everett had reached the bottom of the stairs, most likely. But where was he headed in the middle of the night?

Ned leaned over and snapped his bedside lamp on. His slippers weren't where he had left them against the wall. But it did not matter. As he crept up and tip-toed over to the door, he winced and stopped as he hit a creak in the floor.

There was silence as he listened.

He went as lightly on his feet as he could, lunging for the door. He pulled the door inwards. The hallway was lit with a single lamp on the table further down. Everett's door was closed, as were all of the others. He quietly crossed the threshold and down the hall, and entered the living area. He stopped and listened again, but heard nothing.

Where had Everett gone?

He knew that he couldn't just walk down the creaky stairs like Everett had. As he stood at the top, looking downwards, he saw the

119

wooden rails on either side. Yes, he could balance his weight on those. Get downstairs to the cool marble, where there would be no worry of creaking wood.

But what if Everett were to appear?

How would he explain his straddling the staircase?

He thought for a moment of what he might say. But nothing came to mind.

"It's do or die," he muttered to himself. "Either you want to find out where he's going, or you don't."

And he lifted himself up on the rails.

He guided himself downwards by sliding his palms against the sides of the rail, and kept his feet on the edge of the wooden lip just above the stairs. He shifted himself downwards, bit at a time.

Until he heard a door creak open downstairs.

And then stopped.

He could feel his heart pounding in his chest.

Of course Everett was coming back.

He probably just went to the office to check on something. That had to have been it.

Or maybe get a glass of whiskey from the cabinet behind the desk.

But it didn't matter.

Because Ned decided to wait.

Suspended above the staircase, his legs straddled on the edges of the wooden lips just above the creaky wooden stairs. And he would think of something to say when Everett appeared with his whiskey in hand, appearing around the corner as the ice cubes clanked against the sides of the glass.

But he never appeared.

And the curiosity was reignited.

He still had about half of the staircase to navigate. And below, there was the blue tinted moonlight that had filtered against the cool, white marble floor.

Just a few more steps below.

Should he just draw his legs in and walk down the stairs? Certainly if Everett were just going down to get a drink, he would have certainly reappeared. But now…he must be deeper inside the operation.

But why?

He was the proprietor, of course. But in the middle of the night.

Could he simply not sleep? Was he downstairs, preparing a body?

A clank down the hallway jolted Ned back to the present, standing in the bowels of Waxley. He looked down towards crematory number seven. There was no way that Waxley was down there. But back when Ned had been standing on the staircase, he knew that's where Everett had been.

For he did descend the remaining stairs, and when his feet touched the cold marble, he looked across the foyer and saw the office doors were shut tight.

He crept across the foyer and towards the dark, lengthy hallway that spanned the entire length of the rear side. A sliver of light emitted from the last door. Everett had to have gone down to the basement.

But why?

Ned was compelled to move forward.

The floor was cold and a layer of dust caked on the soles of his feet, but he glided effortlessly down the hall cutting through the impenetrable midnight silence.

He grasped the cool brass handle and pulled the door open just a bit wider, enough for him to see inside. The light was burning. He poked his head inside, around the corner.

The light above the stairs was also burning.

He strained to listen, and could hear clanking. And the *woosh* of a chimney and roar of a fire. Was he cremating someone at this hour?

He rushed down the stairs, entered the receiving room, and saw the door was open. He shivered at the cool night air, and saw the Hearse was running, the headlights shined deeper inside. At the end of the basement hallway, a door was propped open.

And as he stood in the same spot, looking down the same hallway, the same view that he was destined to see, years later, after Mrs. Bannister had visited Waxley, he knew there was something about crematory number seven.

But when he was standing in that spot in the basement for the first time, shortly after he was hired on board, when his curiosity took over, he wasn't aware of any peculiarities that surrounded crematory number seven.

And when he stood in his bare feet, in the dusty shine of the Hearse headlamps, in the middle of the night, he wondered if he should call out to Mr. Waxley. The running Hearse in the middle of the night seemed odd. But he had just come on board, so who was he to question these practices?

Could Mr. Waxley have been called out in the middle of the night?

He certainly could have.

But that wouldn't have explained the running crematorium. He looked down the hallway, and could see a shadow's movement in the light which was reflected on the shiny door. He could emerge from the door at any moment.

And then Ned would have some explaining to do.

He turned and dashed up the steps, emerging in the receiving room upstairs moments later.

He tip-toed down the hall, through the foyer, and up the rickety stairs. He didn't even bother being quiet. There was no way Mr. Waxley would have heard him over the roar of the crematorium.

And as he glided back into his bed, he pulled the sheet back over him and adjusted his pillow. He couldn't get what he saw and heard out of his mind.

A running Hearse.

As he reached to turn out his bedside lamp, he noticed a pen rattling on the wooden table. The rumble was there, but probably wouldn't have woken him had he been sleeping soundly.

And for the remainder of that night, he tossed and turned.

Ned never directly asked Mr. Waxley about cremation chamber number seven.

And the late night cremations continued.

Over time.

Ned remembered waking up in the middle of the night, and in some cases, the living quarters would be whisper quiet and he could hear the sliding doors opening down in the basement receiving area. Or he could look over at the nightstand and see the ripples in a glass of water.

It continued until Ned moved out and found an apartment in a nearby neighborhood.

And for that time period, he had nearly forgotten about the late night cremations.

And much later, after Mr. Waxley had left the mortuary in Ned's control, after a distraught Mrs. Bannister had left, and after Ned had ventured down to the basement level and stood in the receiving area, just as he had in the past when he had lived there, he saw the light emanating through the hallway.

For in those days, when Ned had been in control, he learned of the purpose behind the late night cremations. And the reasoning behind why crematory number seven – and its true purpose – must be preserved.

After Ned had returned from the basement level, he decided that Mrs. Bannister might be a viable candidate to learn about crematory number seven. She was far too distraught to even plan her husband's funeral, and the added revenue that the mortuary would receive should she select the top secret option would be much needed.

But could she sign the contract of lifetime secrecy?

That he would have to determine.

And he knew that Everett Waxley had put him into place at the helm because he had confidence in Ned – that he was capable of making such decisions. He locked the door with a click, as his loafers clapped against the long marble hallway. It was dark outside as he headed across the foyer.

He swung the office doors open and headed towards the painting of Schubert hanging on the back wall. He grabbed the right edge of the massive oil painting and stopped.

He turned around, looking at the expansive desk he had been sitting at when Mrs. Bannister had sat across from him, dabbing her eyes. It was the same chair that he had sat in, across from the very same desk, when he had been called in for an interview.

On that particular day, when Ned had first sat in that office, in the small chair facing the desk, a grandfather clock chimed in the corner of the small, otherwise quiet office.

He sat in front of a small, paunchy man, who held his resume up and studied it, adjusting his glasses. Ned noticed that the man's face was crinkled, and every few minutes, he rubbed his chin and nodded. Ned smoothed his thick, black hair, and wiped a single drop of sweat away that had traveled down the side of his cheek under his dark sideburn. The man across the desk appeared calm, cool and collected.

"Ned McCracken," the man finally said, breaking the silence.

Ned had been fidgeting with his fingers in his lap and raised his eyes when the man spoke.

"Yes," Ned said, with a slight crack in his voice. He cleared his throat. "That is me."

The man raised his eyes and looked at Ned. "You are astoundingly young," he said. "Why do you have such an interest in death at such a young age?"

Ned looked down at the floor and shook his head. He looked back up at Mr. Waxley. "I lost my brother several years ago," he said. "And my father is in the business. I've helped him since I was a young boy. But to answer your question…I suppose I just want to help people."

Ned exhaled and felt the pressure abate.

Then he looked back up at Mr. Waxley. He was smoothing his mustache with his fingertips. Mr. Waxley studied his resume. "I know the McCracken facility up in Detroit. Massive operation."

Ned cleared his throat again and nodded. "It has grown substantially over the past few years, despite the Depression. But yes, I am quite familiar with the facility."

"Hmm…" The man flipped through several pages of Ned's documentation. He paused and looked back up at Ned. "Any relation?"

Ned cracked a thin smile. "That's my father's business."

"Ah, yes." Without looking, Waxley reached over and took a sip from a small, china cup that sat on the desk.

Mr. Waxley leaned back and nodded. "Oh…I see." He flopped the pages on the desk and took another sip from his cup. "So why not continue in the family business? Why are you applying to a funeral home thousands of miles away with a family you have no relation to?"

Ned wiped his palms on the wooden handles of the chair. "I…"

The clock ticked as the man crossed his arms and raised his eyebrows.

He took a breath and exhaled. "I relocated to Miami before my study."

"And you're still not choosing to return to Detroit and assume your father's responsibilities?"

Ned shook his head.

"Why not?"

Ned closed his eyes and pictured the long, barren hallway in the basement. He remembered the green tiles that lined the walls.

And the flickering overhead lights. He could still smell the formaldehyde, the decomposing bodies, as he had remembered walking through the hallway, past preparation rooms, where bodies would lie on large, rectangular tables.

"Mr. McCracken?"

He was brought back to the present and cleared his throat. He shifted in his chair and straightened his back. "I remember it being a very clinical place. I was last there when I was still a boy. And it was always quite unsettling."

The man scoffed.

"How do you think this place will be any different?"

Ned bit his lower lip.

"We're a funeral home, Mr. McCracken. At any given time, we could have up to ten bodies in different rooms…whether it be the embalming and preparation rooms, on display in caskets for viewings, or in receiving from the Coroner…or in the coolers. It's quite clinical here as well. Does death bother you, Mr. McCracken?"

Ned paused for a moment as Mr. Waxley's question hung in the room against the tickling clock.

He could still remember riding his ten speed along the dark, tree-lined side roads not far from the McCracken facility on Telegraph. He could still smell the dust from the sand that had wafted into the air when he slammed to a stop, grinding through the gravel.

He remembered peering into the woods as he saw the dark silhouettes against a pale, blue light through the trees.

"Stephen!" He had called out.

"Mr. McCracken? Are you alright?"

Ned nodded, coming back to the present. "Yes, yes. I am okay."

Mr. Waxley leaned forward. "So let me ask the question again, Ned."

He nodded and wiped his hands on his trousers.

"Does death bother you, Mr. McCracken?"

He sighed. "It did when I was living in Detroit."

"And it doesn't any longer?"

He shook his head. "I've matured and grown over the years. I have a different perspective now."

The man nodded. "Did you become numb? Over the years of being a mortician? Is that how death ceased to bother you?"

Ned shook his head. "No, but I gained a better understanding of it."

Mr. Waxley looked directly at Ned and raised his eyebrows. Ned tugged at his collar. Mr. Waxley said nothing. Maybe he was seeking clarification?

Ned continued. "I was still a teenager when I started working at the McCracken Funeral Home. And that's when I lost my brother. So back then, death bothered me."

"Understandably so. Why would it still not bother you?"

Ned nodded. "I was haunted by his death for years." He shifted in his seat. "But...I believe I have moved beyond that. Since my studies, I have made a commitment – a moral commitment – to help others."

The man cleared his throat but did not look up from the stark white paper. He adjusted his glasses as Ned shook his head, wishing he had gone with cream.

"It says here you studied in San Francisco," he said.

Ned shifted and leaned forward. The man raised his eyes, just for a moment, and looked back down at the paper. "I actually did an apprenticeship out there," he said. "I completed the bulk of my study in Cincinnati."

He raised his eyebrows and set the page down on his desk. He leaned forward for the first time in their lengthy discussion. "Oh…Cincinnati. They are one of the most well respected Mortuary Schools."

Ned nodded. "They are."

"I must honestly say I like that you've been formally trained. I've had candidates in the past come in cold off the street. So you know your way around the embalming room? And the cremation chambers?"

Ned nodded.

"And you understand the science of it all?"

134

Ned relaxed a bit. This is where he felt most comfortable. But he chose to insert a little humor. "The first time I held a trocar in my hands, I had no idea what its purpose was for."

Mr. Waxley's mouth dropped. He set Ned's resume down on the desk, and sat back in his chair with a creak.

The clock ticked in the background.

After a moment, his face shifted. Ned instantly regretted saying that. He should have known better. The trocar was one of the primary tools of a Mortician. He sat in his chair and grasped the wooden arms. He could feel the sweat near his hairline, as he waited for Mr. Waxley to show him to the door.

But he didn't.

Mr. Waxley rose from his chair and started laughing. In the midst of his laughter, he looked over at Ned, his eye's wide. "You what?!"

Ned opened his mouth to speak but nothing came out.

"*That* thing? What the heck did you think it was?"

Ned shifted. Had he escaped? Did his plan of a little humor thaw some of the ice? "I, well…"

Ned tilted his head to the side. "It's just…so…big…and shiny…and…I remember holding it up in front of my face at Mortuary school…and thinking…what the heck is *this* for?! Like…I didn't know that we use it to pierce the carotid artery to push the embalming fluid through a body!"

Mr. Waxley chuckled as he poured himself some coffee from the percolator.

Ned smiled for the first time in the interview.

He returned to the desk and looked at Ned directly. His expression had warmed. "Let me tell you about a common misconception with our field."

Ned nodded. "I'm listening."

Mr. Waxley again stood up, and Ned noticed how large and imposing the man actually was. He stepped backwards considerably to clear his large stomach from the desk, and eased himself over to the other side of the room.

"People generally fear us," he said, as he turned around and faced Ned again. "They think we are all about death. That we're somehow…broken in our minds…to want to choose a field where we are surrounded by dead bodies. And coffins. Graves and such. You know, all the death that surrounds us every day. So people think – at least commonly – that a mortician is about death. But that, really, couldn't be further from the truth. For a mortician, and what we do, is really about life. It's about celebrating a life lived. And having compassion, and caring for those who are still living who have lost their loved one."

"I like your perspective, Mr. Waxley."

He stood at the window, his hands clasped behind his back. "And it's also about legacy. You know, preserving what the dead have left behind for others to remember them. But death…that's just part of our business. And of course it's a part of life. And we are life, Ned."

Mr. Waxley's comments sent Ned back through time.

And then, in his mind, Ned saw a different office. It wasn't the lavish, mahogany laden room as at Waxley's, but a far more modest enclave just across from the main viewing room at his father's much larger operation, which might have been grander in size, but far simpler in appointments.

Still, Ned remembered the McCracken Funeral Home to be a compassionate operation, despite its modesty.

Ned was brought back to the present as Mr. Waxley cleared his throat.

"Ned? Were you daydreaming in the middle of a job interview?"

Ned's heart pounded in his chest as his cheeks grew hot. He shifted his position, leaning forward and adjusting his tie. He let out a single, nervous sounding laugh. "Uh…I'm sorry, Mr. Waxley. It's just…" He looked up at Mr. Waxley, who leaned back against the shelving, and crossed his arms.

There was a soft knock on the door.

"Come in," Mr. Waxley said. Ned turned to see who was at the door. It was a small Hispanic woman. She was wearing a black and white maid's outfit, but conservative, as her black skirt reached down and covered her knees. She clasped her hands in front of her legs and looked down. "The glass workers are here, dear sir."

Waxley gasped. "Oh! They weren't supposed to arrive until tomorrow, am I correct?"

She looked up. "Actually Mr. Waxley, they have been scheduled for today. They want to know if they can start on the viewing room doors."

Waxley nodded and headed back to his desk to retrieve his jacket. "Yes! Of course! I don't know where my mind has been lately." He looked up and over at Ned, who sat, patiently in the chair, watching him conduct his daily business. He pulled his jacket on and raised his eyes towards Ned.

"Would you like to accompany me to the South Viewing Room? We can continue our discussion as we walk."

Ned nodded, rose from his chair, and joined Mr. Waxley, as they exited the heavy, wooden double doors, and stepped on to the marble floors in the foyer. Mr. Waxley paused at the round, mahogany table in the center, just under the hanging crystal chandelier. He grasped the edge of a giant, vibrant green fern that sat in the middle of the table. "Rosa! Please tend to this plant. It seems like its dying."

Ned looked around, but Rosa was nowhere in sight.

As they made their way to the back hallway, Mr. Waxley turned and faced Ned. "The back hallway runs the entire length of the building."

He stepped through a large foyer and through the threshold to the rear hallway. It was brightly lit and was lined with dark, wooden doors, all closed.

Mr. Waxley stood in the center of the hall, just across from the foyer, and gestured to the right. "That way," he said, are our back entrances to the viewing rooms. The front entrances are accessed through the parlor."

He then turned and gestured in the other direction. "That way is the entrance to the preparation rooms. And at the end of the hallway, is the entrance to the lower level, where we have the crematoriums."

Ned raised his eyebrows. "You are performing cremations?"

"Oh yes!" Mr. Waxley said, as they headed towards the viewing rooms down the lengthy hallway. "We are all encompassing. It's the latest thing these days. To get the funerals out of private homes, bring them here, so all of the family's needs are taken care of. From start to finish."

They arrived at the South Viewing Room. Several workers were hauling in large boxes.

"These are the glass workers," Mr. Waxley said. "Stained glass doors are being installed today." Ned looked around the ornate viewing room. Gold painted trim lined both the ceiling walls and the floor. And a large picture window faced the south.

"I designed this building," Mr. Waxley said. "I chose the south view for this room so the sun wouldn't be penetrating the windows at sunset at full force. It would force us to close the drapes. The southern view allows us to keep natural light no matter the time of viewing."

Ned stood in front of the window.

It overlooked expansive, manicured gardens. Colorful flowers. Vibrant green trees. It was the perfect place for a casket.

Mr. Waxley placed his hand on Ned's shoulder and stood next to him, facing the gardens, as the workers behind them tore open wooden crates. "So, Mr. McCracken. When can you start?"

Ned looked over at Mr. Waxley.

He extended his hand. "Welcome aboard, son."

Just a short while after Ned had been hired at the Waxley Mortuary, Mr. Waxley took gravely ill. The illness came on rather suddenly, although some of the staff members thought that Mr. Waxley 'did not look himself' that particular morning when the paramedics had to haul him off to Jackson. And it didn't surprise Ned when he had heard the crash back in the casketing room. When he and Rosa came running, he stopped for just a moment at the threshold, grabbing the sides of the door frame. Rosa screamed and rushed to Mr. Waxley, who was lying on the floor. The casket was nearly knocked off the table, partially hanging off the work table. Mr. Davis was still in the corpse lift apparatus, and his body appeared unharmed. Ned breathed a small sigh of relief.

"Call the medics!" Rosa shrieked. She had dropped her feather duster on the floor and cradled Mr. Waxley's head in her lap. "He is having a heart attack! I can tell! Look at how grey his face looks!"

Ned grabbed the wall phone and dialed the emergency number. Minutes later, the siren wailed outside. Mr. Waxley had fallen unconscious, but when the paramedics were working on him and lifting him onto the gurney, he came to, and reached his arm up towards Ned.

"The Davis…" he was groggy and his speech slurred. "Mr. Davis…"

Ned leaned down. "I will take care of it. I already have Ryan casketing him, and everything is almost set for the viewing. I'll be here to oversee."

"I need you to come to see me..."

Ned nodded. "I'll come after the viewing."

And with that, they whisked Mr. Waxley out the front door and loaded him into the ambulance, but he would never set foot in his funeral home again.

After the Davis viewing, Ned retreated to the office and sat behind the massive, cluttered desk. He fished through his pocket for the business card the paramedics had given him. He got up and went to the phone, the large, wooden box on the wall. He picked up the earpiece from its cradle on the side, and leaned forward towards the mouthpiece. He rang the operator. "Connect me to Jackson Memorial, please."

Ned stood in the hospital hallway as nurses in blue scrubs and doctors wearing white coats darted in and out of the room doors which lined the lengthy hallway. He felt a little out of place in his black suit. He headed forward and smoothed his hair with his hands, and paused at the nurses' station. There was a young assistant sitting at the station, engrossed in a book. Ned stood patiently, watching her read as she slowly turned a page.

He cleared his throat and she raised her eyes, laying her book down on the desk. She flashed a brilliant smile surrounded by bright red lipstick. "How may I help you, sir?"

"I am here to visit Everett Waxley," he said. "He was taken here earlier today by ambulance."

She nodded. "Okay, let me check." She fished through a large stack of papers as Ned shifted from one foot to the other.

"I checked with the emergency department and they said he was admitted here."

She nodded slowly. "Yes…yes. Room 204. Just down that hall to the right. But first, please sign in here." She pointed to a clipboard. Ned signed and headed to his room.

When he arrived in room 204, he saw Mr. Waxley lying in a bed in the middle of the room, surrounded by machines with dials and tubing that ran into his body. There were wires connecting each device to different areas of his body, but mostly his chest area. Ned thought their clinical appearance looked similar to the embalming machines back at the mortuary. Several IV drip bags were hung on tall, aluminum hangers and attached to his arms and wrists.

Mr. Waxley's eyes were closed.

Ned stood at the foot of the bed, watching the man. His face was ashen, his lips scarcely with color. There was no REM movement underneath his eyelids. Just the stone cold sleep of severe illness. Ned stood and watched, until he heard a soft male voice behind him.

"He had a massive stroke, you know."

He turned around and saw a small man in a dark suit sitting at a round wooden table. A fedora hat sat on the table with a leather case. His legs were crossed, and he was leaning over a sea of bright white papers, spread across the table. He slowly removed a pair of silver, wire-rimmed glasses and lay them on the papers. The man stood and adjusted his pants, shifting his suspenders.

"It's amazing he's even still alive," he said, as he took a few steps closer to Ned and extended his hand. "David Gringham," he said. "I serve as attorney for Waxley. He wanted me to meet you here for the transfer."

Ned shook his head and pulled the chair out opposite of David. "Transfer?"

"Of Waxley Mortuary and Funeral Home to you."

Ned flopped in the chair. "To me?"

David nodded, sat back down, and gestured to the paperwork spread across the table. "It's all here. Quite clear. He was preparing this last week."

Ned let out a nervous laugh. "I...I'm not even sure how he could have come to this decision. I mean, I have only even worked for him the last few weeks. And he's leaving his *business* to me?"

Both men looked towards the bed as Waxley coughed. "Tell him...David..." Waxley raised his hand, pointing towards the paperwork. It shook violently, but Ned knew what he was pointing at.

"Tell...him..."

David took a breath and sat back in his chair. He reached down towards the table and organized the papers in a neat pile.

"Okay, Ned. I'm not going to bullshit with you. All this paperwork really has nothing to do with why we are here today. Everett wants you to take over the mortuary because he said he trusts you."

"He trusts me?"

David nodded. "With the business. But also with the secrets of Waxley. And that's why we are *really* here."

Ned raised his eyebrows and leaded forward. "What type of secrets could Waxley hold...given that it's one of the first funeral homes in existence?" He looked over at Waxley. He was lying still, no longer speaking. The medical staff weren't rushing in, so probably just sleeping.

David picked up a legal sized, sealed manila envelope. "Take this with you. I haven't read these documents. But he gave these to me. Read them, and review them. And then we can meet for the signing. Everett has already signed his side. Just waiting on yours."

Ned looked at the envelope as David held it up to him. Ned slowly extended his hand and placed it on the large, sealed envelope, and then looked up at David. Their hands both held the envelope, locked on either side. David didn't yet release his grip, but met eyes with Ned.

"This is meant to be read under extreme secrecy," he said. "Share this with no one."

Ned nodded.

"I mean no one, Mr. McCracken. Especially those who are currently employed by Waxley. These documents are to be kept secure and sacred for as long as you live. And beyond. You will need a trustworthy protégé to pass them to when you are nearing your own death."

David released his grip and Ned looked down at the large envelope, examining it. It looked to be the size of a court room document. And sealed.

"There will be a letter from Everett," David said, rising from his chair and packing his paperwork into his briefcase. "With specific instructions." David headed across the room to the emanating light from the hospital hallway. "When you've reviewed the documents, please give me a call."

And he left the room.

Thunder crashed overhead as Ned pulled the hearse up towards the carport. The mysterious envelope sat on the passenger seat, and he had looked over at it, repeatedly, on the drive from the hospital back to Waxley Mortuary. Once the car was safely parked, he cut the engine, grabbed the envelope, and got out of the car.

He slammed the door, and held the envelope in his hands for a few minutes, staring at it. He held it up to the yellowed light under the wooden carport roof, but could only see the outline of full sized paperwork inside, nothing more.

As he turned to go inside, it was not the paperwork that spoke to him. But his mind.

You are the leader of Waxley now, Ned.

He paused for a moment.

He listened to the gravel laden voice of Everett Waxley, remember the day, just several weeks ago, when he sat across from his expansive mahogany desk.

You will lead the blind to sight...

You will lead the deaf to hearing...

And demystify the mystery of death.

He thought it strange that Mr. Waxley would have leaned back in his high-back, smokey leather chair like he did; sitting there, watching Ned sit in the tiny chair in front of the desk, fidgeting. But at the conclusion of the interview, Ned had looked up at him. His bushy white mustache had concealed his mouth, but he could tell the man was smiling.

But now, standing in the carport, examining the envelope, Ned took a different perspective of how Waxley's eyes had been beyond his mustachioed smile; pleading, beckoning:

I am dying, dear boy. I cannot run this operation without you, dear boy.

He could hear his father's voice reverberate through his mind. The steady, methodic tone. Deep, grating. But determined. He remembered sitting on the chair, watching his father prepare a body for embalming.

He looked over at Ned.

"This is relatively new, Neddie. They've moved away from the arsenic, so it's much safer. But this is the latest technology." He looked over at Neddie and smiled. "I'm glad you're following in my footsteps, son. This is an up and coming business. We're getting funerals out of the homes. And we're bringing them here. That's the way the world is headed."

Ned's mouth dropped open and his arms flopped to his side as he leaned against the wall of the carport. "You *wanted* me to take over since you hired me, didn't you?"

He looked around the carport and there was no answer. Just the pelt of the rain on the metal roof. Only the voice of his father that cluttered his mind.

This is your destiny, Neddie. Your calling.

You were meant to usher the dead to eternal life…

He could see the lamp outside, and the stream of the steady falling rain around the yellow glow of the light.

You were the chosen one…

He fidgeted with the key, and then the door creaked open.

He flicked the bright overhead light on, entering to the receiving room, and there was a black body bag on the preparation table. He gasped. There shouldn't have been any bodies out of the cooler.

"Rosa!" he called. And then he looked at his watch. She would have been long gone at this point. There was a small clipboard with stark white pages on top of the body bag. He placed the manila envelope on the side counter and slowly approached the body bag. He picked up the small clipboard, but the pages were blank.

You will lead them to the light…

Thunder crashed overhead and the lights flickered. He stood, staring at the body lying on the table. There had been no bodies scheduled to be received that day. He knew that much. Just the Davis viewing. And Mr. Davis was safely in his casket, closed and ready in the vestibule, waiting for transport to the church first thing in the morning.

The rain pelted the roof as lighting illuminated the room from outside. He took a step forward and reached out, down to the top of the zipper. He held it steady for a moment.

Pull my zipper down, Ned.

Pull it down and it'll flop out.

He gasped, covering his face with his hands, shaking his head. "No…no…"

His voice was muffled.

"You're not going to find me here…"

But there was no stopping him.

Because Ned knew.

He knew if he pulled that zipper down, Stephen would be there. Lying in the middle of the preparation table; the body bag still the same. The pale green tiles were the same, with the same mosquito carcasses and dried spots of blood. It was the same room. Back when Stephen had been lying on the preparation table.

"You don't get to do this to me again…"

But the night was the same.

Cold and crisp.

Back in the north, and on the same night his mother and father had gotten the call about Stephen. He could still remember his mother collapsing over the kitchen counter.

"No! *No! Not Stephen!*"

But Ned knew.

Ned always knew what happened to Stephen, because of the blue light.

And the zipper.

The whole oxymoron of the zipper was that the zipper was as dark as the day had been bright. And Stephen, the one he had come to trust, his blood, his older brother, didn't come to his aid. He stood with his friends, throwing his head back in laughter.

"Take it you little *faggot!*"

That's all he could remember.

Those words were from Byron, Stephen's friend.

Ned could remember the chill of the Michigan nights when Stephen was still alive. But it didn't matter much after that. After Ned fell back on the ground, the warmth of blood in his mouth, he heard the laughter fade off into the distance. And he knew Stephen was gone, but why hadn't he come to his aid?

And that was the last time he had seen him.

For the next time, as he had been pedaling his 10-speed down Telegraph, when he had stopped with his feet planted in the gravel, under the clear, starlit sky, when he could see each breath, he could hear the screams coming from deep within the forest.

He threw his bike down on the gravel and ran towards the woods. "Stephen!" he called. "I'm coming for you!"

But it didn't matter what Ned thought or did. Because Ned knew, deep in his soul, that he couldn't protect Stephen from his assailant. Because Byron and his friends weren't the ones out there with Stephen. While Ned could hear Stephen's desperate cries for help, the sheer screams against the silence of the forest, his efforts would not matter.

A piercing scream tore against the silence of the night. Ned stopped in his tracks. "Stephen!" He started again, and then was stopped at the edge of the forest, by an unseen veil of pale blue, there was no proceeding. Stephen's screams penetrated his ears but there was no proceeding.

And then Ned saw the walls.

The pale green tiles, and the flickering overhead florescent light.

Stephen, did you come back to me? Did you return to tell me what's beyond? Out beyond the grave?

He looked down at the body bag.

Pat certainly had forgotten about this one. He exhaled, shook his head, and tossed the manila envelope on the counter. He reached around to the body bag, leaning over it and reached for the zipper.

"Let's see what we have here, shall we?"

The tick of the zipper tore against the quiet. The only other sound was the pelt of the rain against the windowpane. The lifeless corpse was revealed. Stark white and bloodless. Stiff. Probably been laying here for a few hours.

But silent.

As the dead should be.

As the dead always have been.

So why was he feeling a sense of anxiety building in the pit of his stomach? Why was a feeling of dread building from within?

I want you to continue...

He stopped and looked up. The window to his right was covered with a blind, but he could see the periodic flash of lightning outside, and the drive of the rain remained.

"We're going to label you as a John Doe if I can't find your receiving paperwork."

Ned completed receiving paperwork for John Doe and unlocked the gurney wheels. He leaned down, and looked at the body one last time. There was something about the man. It could have been his dark mustache. The receding hairline. Or stocky build. But he reminded him of Everett Waxley.

There was just something about him.

He shook his head and jumped as the corpse sat up, with wide eyes.

"You will die here!"

Ned fell backwards onto the floor.

He got up and saw the body flop back onto the table. There was too much similarity. He remembered Stephen doing the same thing. That was too much.

He spilled out into the hallway, and slammed against the tiles on the other side. His head winced, but he didn't wait. He struggled to his feet and hobbled down the hallway.

"Stephen!" he called. His voice reverberated against the concrete walls. "Stephen is still *alive*!" He climbed the stairs, falling on the wooden steps repeatedly, and finally fell against the white hardwood door. "Rosa! *Someone*! Let me up! *Help*!"

And he spilled into the North Viewing Room. There was a lamp on in the adjacent hallway, but the remainder of the room was dark. For a few minutes, he lay on the floor, the side of his face against the carpet, his eyes closed. There was too much here. Too much in this business.

And too many memories of Stephen.

He covered his eyes with his palms and whimpered.

The night felt the same, back at McCracken.

He could still remember walking into the kitchen at his childhood home, walking in and seeing his mother crying on his father's shoulder.

She was sobbing as he embraced her and rubbed her back. Mother looked up when Ned came in. Her eyes were red rimmed and the mascara was running down her cheeks in a network of spider veins.

"Oh honey," she said. She loosened from Father's embrace and he turned. Ned saw that he had also been crying.

"Honey, come over here," mom said, her voice quivering. She sniffled and held her arms out. "Your brother died last night."

He could feel the skin on this sides of his face tighten. And he heard the screams from the forest replay in his mind, over and over.

His face felt hot, and as he rested his head against his mother's bosom, he could feel her heartbeat. He closed his eyes.

But he could also feel his own racing heart. His breath came quick and shallow, and he tried to close his eyes, but the tears still bellowed in his eyes.

Ned awoke to a pounding headache and the running of a vacuum cleaner in a faraway room. He saw the first fingerlings of sun feel their warmth through the sliver of curtains, and in the darkness, he could make out the shadow of the coffin. What time was it? Certainly he had not slept on the floor all night long?

He felt the ache in his back as he struggled to his feet, feeling much older than his years. The floor had not been an inviting bed, and he wished he hadn't passed out there. He would certainly pay for it the rest of the day. He looked up as the doors on the opposite wall slid open with a bang, flooding the viewing room with light.

Rosa gasped, pushing in her vacuum cleaner. "Oh Mr. McCracken! You are down here already? I'm so sorry. I didn't know. I didn't see you."

He shook his head and waved his hand. "No, no Rosa. It's fine." He pinched the corners of his eyes next to his nose. "What time is it, Rosa?"

"It's twenty to ten."

Ned gasped. "Almost ten o'clock?! How did I sleep so late?!" He rushed over to the casket and opened the lid. Declan was still lying there peacefully. He'd died with his eyes open. Ned noted the tiny stitches held fine. He'd never been that great with a needle and thread.

But this time, it looks like he scored one.

You're sleeping mighty late there, Declan. You care for a cup of coffee to rouse you?

Ned closed his eyes and shook off the sleepiness. There wasn't much time to prepare. Family would be arriving in just a few minutes, and the guests not much after that. He reached down and picked up a flower arrangement and placed it on a pedestal next to the casket. Rosa was running the vacuum when he turned around.

"I have to freshen up!" he called. "At least clean my teeth or something!"

She stopped the vacuum and fished the plug out of the outlet. "And your suit sir. There's a stain on the leg."

He looked down. She was absolutely right. It was white, faded. But noticeable. And then he slapped his forehead.

"What's wrong sir?"

"This is just not my day," he said, shaking his head. "I left the John Doe on the table downstairs." And then he lowered his voice, speaking under his breath. "He's been there all fucking night."

She tilted her head to the side after she finished wrapping the cord around the vacuum cleaner. "John Doe?"

He closed his eyes, shook his head, and sighed. "The body that came through last night. I left it on the table and forgot to place it in the cooler."

She shrugged her shoulders and started to push the vacuum cleaner towards the sliding doors to the foyer. "No bodies last night, Ned. It was an unusually slow night."

He froze as he felt the sides of his face tighten again. He stood next to the door marked PRIVATE.

Through that door, the door that was discreetly placed like a secret passage through the castle, nestled between massive, gold-framed oil paintings and behind a floor standing fern, was the entrance to the hallways with the green tiles.

And the bloody mosquito carcasses.

He looked back over towards the foyer doors and saw Rosa was gone. He called out. "You sure, Rosa?"

"Yes," she called back. "I clocked out just after you left to visit Mr. Waxley. And there's nothing on the log this morning."

Ned took a few steps towards the door and extended his hand, poised just a few inches from the brass knob, ready to open and turn, and stopped.

He could feel his heart beating.

And he could hear some piano music playing, wafting in the background. It sounded distant and muffled. Next Rosa would set the lighting and all would be ready.

Except for him.

Because he could not thaw his hand.

It was locked in front of the knob, ready to grasp, ready to turn, but powerless. Until he heard Rosa's voice.

"Ned!" she called. "Only ten minutes!"

He snapped out of it and shook his head.

He grasped the handle, flung the door open, and tore down the stairs. He saw the light at the end of the dark cement hallway. Of course he had left the light on. And the body would be lying right there. Hard as a fucking rock. Probably already starting to stink.

He stopped at the threshold and his mouth dropped.

The table was empty.

But there was no time to speculate. He snapped the light off and headed further down to the door at the end of the hallway, and took the massive coffin elevator up to the display room, and cut through to the door marked PRIVATE behind several display caskets, and sneaked into his private quarters via the hidden staircase. There simply had been no time. The family would be arriving any minute. And he looked a mess.

He dashed through his modest living room – sparsely furnished with plain furniture, no artwork on the walls, and into the bedroom and tore off his suit, ripping off the shirt. He heard the buttons flying into the walls with a soft *tink!* and then he undid his belt.

He reached in the closet for a new shirt when the phone rang. It slowed him down, at least for a few minutes. He let out an exasperated sigh as he lifted it off the wall and yanked it up to his ear. He dodged the cord as he fished his underwear from his legs and around under his feet.

"Yeah? Pat?"

Of course it was Pat.

Calling from the office.

And of course the family was already arriving. Ned looked over at the clock, and the big hand was on the three. Quarter past. So of course the family was arriving. Because their guests would be arriving in fifteen minutes.

"The body's ready," Ned said, rummaging through his drawers for some Veldoni knickers.

He yanked them out and pulled them up, as they bushed around his waist like loose fitting shorts. "Rosa has the music on. Just let them in and they can spend some time with Declan. I'll be down in less than five."

The line was silent until Ned looked up. "Uh, hello?"

"I'm here," Pat said.

"Okay…so you heard what I said, right?"

"Yeah, I heard it. I have Rosa showing them into the room now. But what happened to *you*, Ned? You're never late for these things."

Ned closed his eyes and sighed.

Images of the woods and the sound of the zipper flashed through his mind.

"Look," he said. "I've had a very...weird...night after I got back from the hospital. Just give me five minutes to get myself in a fresh suit and I'll be down there."

"Okay," Pat said, with a note of reluctance in his voice. "I mean...everything appears to be under control. But the family has already asked for you, and you know how that is..."

"Yes, yes, I know. I planned this one. But you're perfectly capable of running the show."

"That I am."

Ned nodded as he pulled the underwear on, holding the phone between his neck and shoulder, and tucking his penis in the pouch just as he had since he was a boy. He held the phone back up to his ear and looked at himself in the mirror. He looked clean. His chest was hairless and pasty white, yet slim and fit, as he always had been. He lifted his arm and stuck his nose next to his armpit. "I just need five minutes," he said. "I will be right there."

Ned stripped off the fresh knickers and decided to hop in the shower since Pat was downstairs getting the family situated. He knew it would have to be a record-time washing since he knew that any minute the phone would be ringing again if he didn't show his face downstairs.

But the phone didn't ring.

And when the hot water was warming his skin, and he felt the warmth run over his cheeks, he reached down toward his lower abdomen, and ran his fingers over the scars. The firm skin gave way to the line of rough, protruding tissue. But it was still there. After all those years.

And the screams pierced his thoughts again. And thoughts of how Stephen would defend him, as much as he could, up until the last time, when Bryon assaulted him. But it was Bryon who Ned had thought was his friend.

For when Ned stood in the shower, the water cascading down around his head and neck, dripping downwards over his arms, he stared at his penis.

And that made him think of Bryon.

And the zipper.

That day had been so many years ago, but he had thought, back then, that Bryon had been a friend. And at least then, he was. They spent their days together shooting hoops and getting sweaty. It was the peak of summer, and Ned couldn't help but stare when Bryon peeled off his shirt, his tanned muscular torso glistened in the searing sun.

He looked over at Ned, who stood, stammering, making every attempt to look away. "Take off your shirt man," Bryon said. "It's hot as hell out here."

Ned pulled up his shirt and tossed it on the ground but wished he hadn't.

Bryon was older, taller, more muscular, and not pasty white like Ned was. Bryon was one of the guys who always seemed to have an ongoing tan regardless of the time of year.

Ned reached over and shut the water off from his shower with a squeak. He grabbed a towel and rubbed it over his skin. No more trips down memory lane. He had to get downstairs. But even as he pulled his knickers back on, he kept on thinking of Bryon. It had been years since he had seen him, and the last he had heard, the young man died from a bad case of the mumps.

After Declan's family visited and cried over his casket, and after the last guest had left, Ned stood over the coffin and folded the satin liner inwards. He heard footsteps approaching but didn't need to turn around.

"Can you help me with the lid?" He turned and Pat was standing beside him. Ned finished folding the satin inwards and gave it a light pat. He bent down and grabbed the head side of the lid. He looked up and around his shoulder as Pat grabbed the foot end. They hoisted it up and placed it on the casket as the doorbell chimed.

They adjusted the lid as Rosa's heels clapped against the stone floor of the foyer. As Pat adjusted the coffin lid, Ned stood back and looked on.

Could he be a worthy successor? Could Pat be trusted with the knowledge of what goes on with crematory number seven?

Ned loosened his tie and removed his jacket.

There was a lot to consider.

The time he had spent with Mr. Waxley had solidified a bond. Pat was friendly, efficient, and clearly well versed in the operations of a mortuary…but he didn't know if Pat was ready for the insider information.

As the sun started to set in the South Viewing Room, Ned walked through, carrying his jacket over his shoulder, and stopped in front of the stained glass gates that Mr. Waxley had installed when he had interviewed some time ago.

The man had certainly known about opulence.

And the small details, like keeping the largest window opening to the gardens, and in a location that would prevent the harsh intrusion of a sun lowering in the sky, set Mr. Waxley apart from the other Funeral Directors.

Ned headed for the back stairs.

As he climbed the creaky, wooden stairs, his jacket still over his shoulder, he ran over the next day's events.

Declan was scheduled to be entombed in a crypt right over in Resurrection. And the procession was to start shortly.

It was a real nice plot, Ned thought. Right by a large oak. Not far at all. Close walk, both directions. But the hearse would be used, in traditional standard, of course. No carrying of the coffin.

And after the burial, when Ned sat in his small kitchenette, his cat approached and rubbed up against his leg. The day's work was finished.

He poured himself a glass of whiskey, and reread the letter that Mr. Waxley had given him in his final days:

Ned,

When you first interviewed for the role of Assistant Mortician, I initially thought you weren't planning on remaining in Miami for very long, with your family business being cross country in southern Michigan.

While I was surprised that you weren't planning on following in your Father's footsteps in the McCracken Funeral Home, I also understand and empathize with the reasoning behind your decision.

In the subsequent period after your interview and resulting hire, as you know, we had many discussions about your aspirations, your past and history. And also the legacy that you desire to leave behind when you leave this world. I appreciate how we have grown close in such a short period, and I must honestly say, I have come to trust you implicitly.

So, Ned, I write you this letter after learning that my health has been on a steady decline.

One cannot manage a busy Funeral Home, Cemetery and Mortuary indefinitely. It's unfortunate for myself that I am the last remaining Waxley family member. But it is time for me to move forward.

And so, with you now my closest confidant, in the event of a further decline of my health, I plan to have you assume full control of Waxley.

In anticipation of my death, I am having my attorney draw up the formal documents which you and I will both need to sign. It will transfer full ownership of Waxley at the moment of my death.

After I have died, my attorney has instructions as my executor. My body will be returned to Waxley and prepared by you and you alone. There are stringent specifications as to how you are able to handle my body after I have died. I cannot be embalmed. I must be washed, dressed, placed into a casket and into cremation chamber number seven.

It must be number seven — no other.

And it must take place within one day after my death. After the sun sets on the second day, it will be too late.

As you know, a large oil painting of the mortuary hangs behind my desk in the administrative offices.

That painting frame is hinged from the wall, and with the key that is located in my right hand drawer in a small niche near the back, you will be able to unlock the frame and it will be able to swing outwards from the wall. That will reveal the storage location for the documents that you must protect.

You must protect them with your life and tell absolutely no one about their existence or their contents.

But should you find the operation in a financial need, should someone be properly vetted, the services offered by cremation chamber number seven can be offered at a super-premium price.

With regards to who you find to assist you, you must find someone you can trust completely to hand the documents down to in the event of the decline of your health or demise, as this is the only way to protect Waxley.

Further instructions will await you behind the painting.

Please realize that you will only be reading this letter in the event of a serious decline in my health to the point of incapacitation, and you will only gain access to the documents in the event of my death.

Like the stain of colored glass, I trust that the details of your artistry will always be in the most noble of intentions.

I am certain that you will guard the legacy of Waxley with your life.

And in the event of your impending death, I trust you will choose a worthy successor.

In Secrecy,

Everett T. Waxley

Proprietor

Waxley Mortuary and Funeral Home

THE SÉANCE

THOU SHALL NOT ATTEMPT contact of the dead.

And if thou shall, then they will open themselves up to peril; and great torment. For the dead are silent. If they speak, they do not use words. And those who do speak are rarely, if ever, the spirit which was sought for communication.

Moments come to fruition.

Feelings wash over those in rooms and hallways that the dead were purported to have a connection. Places where a single, solitary object might usher memories into a mind which had come close to forgetting after years and decades.

The dead do communicate.

But rarely with words.

And those who ignore the directive, those who venture into the world of deathly communication, most often find themselves contacting spirits, yes, but in many cases, not speaking with their deceased loved ones.

The group of students had initially agreed to meet in the University Mall after classes had ended for the day. After class, Jacob again sat on the steps to the library, a camera dangling around his neck. Like Darryl had said, it was too hot that day for the jeans he was wearing, and he longed for a pair of shorts. He could feel the moisture on the back of his knees. He lifted his palm from the cover of his spiral notebook, noticing the wet imprint it left. As he saw Darryl approach him, a drip of perspiration traveled down his back.

Earlier that day, before class, when Darryl had nodded as he approached and Jacob stood. "We have to change," Jacob said. Darryl nodded, but didn't otherwise recognize Jacob's request. And they met with Susan, ran into Professor Howell, went to class, and there had been an unofficial agreement to meet again in the afternoon after classes, or so Jacob thought.

But in the afternoon, Susan and Darryl never came, and even when Jacob was messaging them, there was no reply. He knew what the answer had been; they had given it to him before. Had they been just trying to appease him? But as the sun reached a lower point in the sky, and he hadn't seen his research partners, he knew it was time. As he got up and headed down the cement steps, he approached his waiting 4x4 truck. He knew they weren't going to come with him. But that one last ditch effort made him feel like more of a friend.

The drive across town to Waxley Mortuary was uneventful. And as he pulled down the desolate Ascension Avenue, he approached the pothole laden, forgotten dead-end of the street where the Mortuary sat next to Resurrection Cemetery along the side of the cracked and broken sidewalks.

It was the forgotten section of town, which was for certain. Shaded by a gigantic oak tree canopy, the heat of the Florida sun was filtered significantly; the sun only reached the ground in patches.

Jacob cut the engine to his 4x4 and waited on the side of the road. He looked in the rearview mirror and saw the daylight fading through the thick forest of trees that lined the desolate two-lane road.

In the front of the truck were the wrought-iron gates, rusted from decades of neglect.

The entrance to Waxley Mausoleum looked vastly different than it had earlier in the day, in the bright sunlight, when Jacob had visited it the first time.

He swung the truck door open with a creak and he hopped out. He slammed shut with a thud against the otherwise silent twilight. His heart started beating faster as he took several steps closer to the gate. Bits of displaced gravel on the pavement crunched with each step.

He fished his phone out of his pocket as the screen livened and cast a glow against his face. It was nearly time. He looked back around his shoulder; the truck was parked facing him, now looking darker in the silhouette of the fading light and towering, shadowy forests that lined the lonely road.

He shoved his phone back into his front pocket and reached out and touched the rusted gates.

He looked up at the towering cement columns on either side of the gates and felt a chill run through his spine. He yanked his fingers back.

Trash littered the broken pavement.

It looked like it had been decades since this stretch of Ascension had been repaved. This section of the street probably was just as old as Waxley itself, given the state of the disrepair.

Jacob looked up at the sky as the late afternoon clouds meandered by. The sun would be setting soon. It had felt much cooler in the shade of his 4x4, and as he fished a Salem from his breast pocket. He loosened and removed his red tie – the red tie he wore since it was a Tuesday. As he blew out a cloud of smoke, he turned his head to the right and looked at the old, dilapidated markers of Resurrection Cemetery, through the equally dilapidated, and rusted, wrought-iron fence. All the mounds of dirt were still there, untouched for decades.

He then looked down at the paperwork he was holding.

Mysterious Local Cemetery Houses No Bodies

And the local ghost tour pamphlets that touted the phenomenon. Where were the bodies?

Somehow the tour company had received permission from the city to conduct ghost tours in the cemetery, but he'd read that the mortuary itself was off-limits, due to numerous hazards inside.

Earlier, after the class where he, Darryl and Susan declared their thesis statements, and as the other students were filing out the front door, Professor Howell had pulled Jacob aside.

He held Jacob's arm, squeezed it a bit, and looked down, directly in his eyes.

"Listen, Jacob," he said. "Waxley was my project too. That's the only reason I approved it. I want to see if the three of you can go in there, investigate, and find out more than my group did. But there's one thing that you need to find, which I never did."

Jacob looked up at Professor Howell. His face was expressionless, but he continued to hold Jacob's arm.

"What was that?"

Professor Howell released his grip and straightened his posture. "It has to do with Resurrection Cemetery. And why the bodies have all disappeared. Have you ever wondered that, Jacob?"

Jacob stared into Professor Howell's eyes.

Jacob shrugged his shoulders. "Sure. I hadn't heard a whole lot about that part though."

Professor Howell scoffed and shook his head. "So you are leaving out one of the most important mysteries of the Waxley Mortuary then. Aren't you?"

Jacob stammered. "I…"

Professor Howell raised his eyebrows and nodded. Jacob looked up at his smug look.

"Then you have," he said.

Jacob sighed, closed his books, and shoved them into his backpack.

"Wait a minute," Professor Howell said.

The last remaining students left the room as Professor Howell returned to the instructor's desk and packed up his materials into a small, leather messenger bag. He slung it over his shoulder and joined Jacob at the door. "So you are planning on going tonight, right?" He looked down at Jacob as they exited to a busy hallway with students darting in various directions.

"Uhhh…you told me not to."

Professor Howell chuckled and threw his head back. "I'll go with you," he said. "I knew you were going to go anyway. Best you don't go alone."

Jacob's eyes widened and he looked up at him. "You?"

He nodded. "Yes. Me."

Professor Howell stopped at a door marked THEOLOGICAL STUDIES and turned back to face Jacob. "It won't be a university sponsored research trip, of course. But this is a major stone that I left unturned with *my* thesis, and I would like to investigate it myself."

Jacob nodded slowly. "Well I *was* planning on going there myself tonight. Darryl and Susan sort of said they might come."

Professor Howell nodded and scoffed again as he swiped his card and opened the door to a bay of offices. "Which could possibly get you barred from presenting this topic to the committee because it would be unauthorized research of a city location. But with me there, I will make sure that doesn't happen."

"Doesn't this pose as a risk to you?"

He nodded. "Yes. I could lose my tenure. But like I said…I will work to make sure that this doesn't happen. As far as the university is concerned, this trip will never have happened. No matter what happens. Deal?"

Jacob nodded.

That evening, as he waited next to his truck, he wondered if Professor Howell had been pulling a fast one. Jacob flicked his lighter and listened to the crackle of a second cigarette as he inhaled. As he blew out a cloud of smoke, he heard the crunch of gravel as footsteps approached from behind him. He turned and saw Professor Howell, but it didn't look like the same Professor from the school. His normally styled hair was dry and mussed. He was wearing a white tank top and faded jeans. He looked like they could be friends. Not as far apart in age as Jacob had thought. And for the first time, he noticed Professor Howell as a man and not just an instructor.

"Jacob!" he called.

He removed his sunglasses as he stood next to Jacob. He watched as he hooked the shades in the neck of his tank top, and couldn't help but notice that Professor Howell had a pretty meaty and muscular chest. Defined arms.

He clearly knew his way around the weight room.

He noticed Jacob noticing and when Jacob's eyes raised, they made eye contact.

"Yes, Jacob?"

"I couldn't help but notice your chest," he said. "I had no idea you were so fit."

Professor Howell chuckled and set his backpack on the ground. "Well, you see me at work," he said. "This is me *not* at work. I'm just a regular guy, like yourself. I watch sports. I work out. I chase after women." He leaned in closer towards Jacob, his eyes nearly closing to slits. "In fact, I don't think we're that far apart in age…"

"But what about the grey hair?"

Professor Howell laughed. "You don't think guys can go prematurely grey?" He tossed his head back and laughed again.

Jacob stamped his cigarette out on the pavement, examining Professor Howell's face more closely. The man actually looked young in the face, despite the shoulder length silver hair. "Actually no, seeing you now, I don't think we are. Maybe a few years?"

Professor Howell nodded. "If that. And call me David."

"Okay, David." He looked over at the Mortuary, which was darkening increasingly in the fading sun. "So what is first?"

David picked his backpack back up and placed it on his shoulders. "Well, first we look through the offices. Because the clue as to why there are only mounds of dirt in the cemetery over there are going to be in that office, if anywhere."

Jacob nodded as David stood, facing the mortuary, his hands firmly planted on his hips.

"Profess – er, *David*...I mean," Jacob stammered. "Ha ha...sorry about that David."

David turned around and cracked a half smile.

"What are you looking for?" Jacob asked.

David took a deep breath and let it out. He bent down and picked up his bag and shook his head. "It's something I had been looking for with my own thesis, but didn't find. You see, the difference for me is I never got the chance to go through the office. But there's paperwork in there that is supposed to hold clues about the cemetery. And why there are no bodies there."

Jacob looked through a break in the wall. He saw the tilted, weathered markers. The crumbled mounds of dirt. And the overgrowth of the grounds, which appeared to be untended for years, if not decades.

"The city stopped caring for the grounds since there were no bodies there. It's like it's just a group of cenotaphs, now."

Jacob stubbed his cigarette out on the sidewalk with the toes of his boot. "So what happened to the bodies?"

David smacked his forehead, and turned around to face Jacob. "*That's* what we are going to try to find out. I'm here to help you. I never found this out when I did my thesis. We're going to find out for yours. And that will get yours published."

Earlier in the day, before he and Professor Howell, which he was getting to know simply as 'David', met in front of the Waxley Mortuary and Resurrection Cemetery, Jacob sat in class waiting to gain the University's permission to conduct thesis research for a previously researched topic.

He furiously scribbled notes on his three ring binder as Professor Howell announced the class thesis project assignment groups. Professor Howell pressed the wall button and raised the projection screen as Jacob slammed his notebook shut and looked forward.

Professor Howell raised his eyes as some of the other students looked back in his direction.

Professor Howell walked to the small desk in the front of the room, picked up his messenger bag, and tossed it on the front instructor's desk. "So you want to investigate Waxley?"

Jacob sat back in his chair as Professor Howell and the other students looked at him, waiting.

Jacob nodded. "Yes. Yes, I do."

Professor Howell looked at the two students in the front row. Susan sat next to Jacob, and had been tying her hair back behind her head. She turned around and looked at Jacob, who shrugged his shoulders. She snapped back around and looked up at Professor Howell.

"That's fine," she said. "I'll do it."

"And the third member of your group?"

Jacob cleared his throat. "Darryl. Darryl Coleman." Jacob turned around.

Darryl raised his head and nodded. "I'm in," he said.

Jacob felt a sigh of relief.

Professor Howell looked down at Jacob, smiled, and looked at him directly. "Then you have your research group. Congratulations, you can make your thesis statement to the board."

Jacob and David made their way towards the towering, rusted wrought-iron gates that hung haphazardly outwards towards the cracked sidewalks.

Shrubberies that may have once been glorious and blooming stood unkempt and wildly growing with broken branches and rotting leaves.

"So the Waxley home has been abandoned for several decades now," David said. "Mr. Waxley had fallen ill, was hospitalized and died of a stroke quite suddenly. Now, the Waxley Mortuary had been in the family for decades, but the proprietor then, Everett Waxley, had no living relatives to leave the business to. So he opted to leave it to his most trusted associate, a mortician he had hired named Ned McCracken, even though Ned had only worked at the mortuary for a short time."

Jacob looked up at him and raised his eyebrows. "So there were two morticians here?"

David's head shifted back and forth as they parted overgrown and dead foliage and approached the dilapidated building. "Not…exactly. Only for a short time, really."

"How so?"

"Well, after Everett died, he left the Waxley Mortuary to Ned McCracken, who was recognized, at least at the time, as a stellar Mortician. But not long after Everett passed, Ned went missing."

"He went missing?"

David nodded as they reached a clearing near the funeral home. "There were rumors. Some thought he died, others thought that there was a connection between the missing bodies and Ned's disappearance."

The rusted wrought-iron gate squeaked as David pulled it open. Jacob stood at the threshold and looked up at the old building, noticing the dead shrubberies and broken trees that surrounded the path.

David pushed his way forward.

"Let me lead the way," he said. "I know a safe way in."

Jacob nodded and followed.

As they crunched through the bed of decayed leaves and fallen twigs, Jacob hoisted his backpack from one shoulder to the other. David was looking up and ahead, focused on the Mortuary.

"So why the change of heart?" Jacob asked.

David stopped and turned around. "I told you," he said. "When I was here, I left one stone unturned. And we have to find it. We're gonna start with the office."

Jacob shrugged his shoulders and nodded. They crunched forward, and came to a clearing. "You know, I've been here before," Jacob said. David snapped his head around. "You have?"

Jacob nodded.

"Years ago. I was still basically a kid. We never went inside the building, but went and explored the cemetery."

David shook his head. "It's amazing you didn't get hurt. There's a lot of stories around this plot of land."

"Which stories?"

David pressed forward. "Like that Mr. Waxley chose it from being sacred ground. Where rituals were performed hundreds of years ago."

"What kind of rituals?"

"For those seeking resurrection of the dead."

Jacob felt a chill run through his spine.

A flash of the weathered mounds of dirt flashed through his mind.

David walked through the bed of fallen leaves that led up to the edge of the brick and mortar. He stopped just short of a broken, boarded window.

Yellowed, tattered drapes blew outside the opening.

"Hey!" Jacob called. "So what is the deal with these so called secret documents?"

David huffed and turned. "Look. I have completed years of research on this place. And Ned McCracken. And the entire scandal surrounding this place." He pointed across the yard and through the woods. Jacob looked over and saw the grave markers.

David spun around to face Jacob. "Do you know what the deal is with there being no bodies in that cemetery?"

Jacob shook his head.

"Exactly," David said. He turned and walked a few steps closer to Jacob. "When I was researching *my* thesis of this place, I discovered that, when Everett Waxley lay dying in a hospital, the deed to the business was signed over to Ned McCracken. *And*…Ned was told that there were secret documents that he was supposed to guard with his life."

"How do you know this?"

"Let's just say I've spent a lot of time here," he said. He gestured back to the building. "And have had conversations in there that have led me to believe that the files still exist, somewhere in there."

"What makes them so secret?"

David shrugged his shoulders as Jacob looked up at the crumbling bricks on the corner of the towering building.

The mortuary was in a sad state.

It looked like an old, dilapidated Victorian mansion against the dim sky. Jacob thought back to his research on the construction: a combination of brick, nestled with wooden Victorian windows. The wood frame construction had been unusual for those parts of Florida, especially in more recent times, but the solid turn-of-the-century workmanship, as Mr. Waxley would always say, "could withstand any storm that nature set forth!"

The wooden window borders, though, when they approached it, were faded, cracked and broken. The years of neglect had taken a toll. There was a large, gaping hole on the north side which, if one were to approach it through the overgrown gardens, they could see inside.

Most of the windows were broken.

Jacob saw tattered and yellowed shears blowing outwards in the passing breeze from the first floor window to the left of the main entrance.

"That was his office," David said, as they traversed the side of the building, heading towards the *porte cochere*.

There were those who thought it had been a funeral home in a past life. But for the residents who lived close by, there were other darker, more sinister thoughts

David headed up the crumbled stairs to the massive front porch. "Some believe the documents you were mentioning hold the answer to where the bodies have gone." David reached for a massive, rusted door handle and pulled. The door cracked open to darkness. He turned around as Jacob navigated the broken steps and joined him on the front porch.

"You've been doing your research, right?"

Jacob scoffed and scowled. "Yes, of course I have! What type of graduate student do you think I am?!"

David turned to look at Jacob, his eyebrows raised. Jacob stood, facing David, holding his backpack, looking up at the man. Jacob noticed that his facial hair, while closely cropped, was more of a salt-and-pepper look. David held the door open, just at a crack. Jacob craned his neck around, but saw nothing.

David straightened his posture and looked down at Jacob. "So what's your theory on the cemetery?"

"My…theory?"

David nodded. And then waited as Jacob stammered. "You haven't made the connection, have you?"

Jacob looked up at David, who stood, waiting. After a few minutes, he shrugged his shoulders, turned, and creaked the door open to darkness.

David shook his head. "Just come on," he said.

He stepped up to the threshold.

The door creaked open to darkness.

Some dust billowed out as David waved it away from his face. "It's been nearly a decade since my thesis."

"A whole decade?"

David cracked a smile. "I went right after my undergrad. You've been working for a while?"

Jacob nodded.

He craned his neck to see around David and peered into the darkness. It was just as he had imagined it. Like he was stepping back in time. As he crossed the threshold, he could even smell the change in the air; there was a certain scent to the air.

Like it was old.

Not bad, not noxious or lethal.

Just…old.

He closed his eyes.

The air certainly contained an odor, but Jacob could not place it.

Not necessarily unpleasant, but not one he had recognized. One that he had not smelled before, but he was certain that it was adherent to this funeral home. As if it were air, trapped inside the building, from a bygone era, experienced by those who had inhabited the funeral home so many years in the past.

As Jacob took several steps inside he heard David behind him. "I'm gonna prop the door open. Sun's going down fast."

Jacob opened his eyes.

In the fading light that emanated from the front door, he saw David's dark silhouette dragging an old, dusty side chair across the foyer. He placed it on the porch in front of the open door, holding it open.

Jacob stood and looked over at a set of stairs that wound around the edge of the foyer. As he looked upwards, and his eyes followed the staircase up towards the soaring ceiling and the second floor, he saw the broken rafters blocking access to the upper level.

"Roof caved in back in the eighties," David said. He handed Jacob a high powered flashlight. Jacob nodded and snapped it on.

The foyer was once grand.

He looked down at the marble floors, covered with crumbled plaster, broken wood, shattered glass.

There was a large, round wooden table in the center of the foyer. The wood was permeated with rot; crumbling. Perhaps termite infested. But its intricate carvings on the legs proved that it was once an elegant, artistic piece of furniture. He took a few steps forward and stopped.

"David?"

He turned around.

The door was still propped open, but David wasn't there. No footsteps.

Jacob shined his flashlight on the wall to his left. There was a set of double wooden doors next to a large, oval mirror.

A door slammed in the far hallway.

He gasped and aimed his flashlight forward. He saw the hallway that ran off the back of the foyer. "David?" His voice reverberated against the silence.

He set his flashlight on the wooden table in the center of the foyer. The yellow circle of light emanated across to the far hallway and shined against the wall.

He cupped his hands around his mouth. "David! Where did you go?!"

Another door slammed.

From deeper in the building, down the hallway, for sure.

He turned around as he heard a crash and wood splintering.

The chair flew across the foyer as the front door slammed and covered him in darkness.

Oh, Jacob...

Are you ready?

Are you ready for my bag and my zipper?

He froze.

His flashlight, the only source of light in the pitch black, shone against the far hallway.

Come deeper within…

He reached for his flashlight without looking down at the table. His eyes, transfixed on the hallway ahead, the circle of faded yellowed light shining against the far wall in the dim surroundings, ushered him further into the mortuary. He turned around one last time.

Should he try the door?

He shuffled across the debris on the dusty marble floor.

Locked.

"David?"

He called out one last time against the silence, but there was no answer. Where had David gone?

He ventured further in.

Back towards the long hallway, with an entrance on the far end of the foyer, the length running perpendicular. He paused at the threshold, and shined his flashlight to the left.

He saw a door on the opposite wall, but darkness ahead.

He snapped around and shined his flashlight in the opposite direction. There was a hint of light at the far end. Perhaps from an opening. But there wouldn't be light there for long. The sun was almost completely over the horizon.

"David?"

Still no answer.

He turned to the right and headed towards the faded light. He shuffled his feet along the flooring, unsure of where debris may possibly trip him. As he ventured further into the darkness, he paused.

Was there music?

An organ?

The indistinct light at the end of the darkened hallway seemed warmer than before. Not quite so much like fading daylight. More of a tint. And then he caught his breath in his throat.

I have a banana for you little Jacob...

He could feel his heart pound in his chest as he got closer to the light.

And the music.

There was organ music playing in the distance. Yes, that's what it was.

This couldn't be real. He closed his eyes for a moment, pinching the crest of his nose. And then he looked down the hallway again. And the light still emanated from the slit under the door; the muffled organ music still played.

From far back in the rooms, he could hear it as his heart thumped harder and his breath caught in his throat.

As he got closer, and stood just outside the door, he saw the light emanate from underneath a closed door: it was the color of roses, and he could hear shuffling, the organ music, and the faint waft of voices.

He reached out and grasped the doorknob. Brass, cool, still in perfect condition after so many years.

And he turned.

David retreated into the office as Jacob made his way towards the back hall. David didn't notice that the door pulled shut behind him. The office was just as he'd left it a decade previously – the desk was still sitting in the center of the room. It was far more weathered and worn; the wood was crumbling at the corners; intruding moisture, mold, possible infestation. But it was otherwise intact and in the exact same place it had been.

Jacob thought that David *hadn't* entered this office back when he was conducting his research, but actually, he had. Back in those days, there had been a different aura surrounding the research. There had been no discussion of bodies that had failed to populate nearby graves. There was simply the question of Ned McCracken's mysterious disappearance.

But the question of Ned's disappearance remained, and the Waxley Mortuary lay in ruins, and Ned was still missing, most likely now deceased due to the time that has passed.

Since his research mission, David had learned about the Schubert painting.

He hadn't known that in the year of his own research, and during the time of his initial research, David had rummaged through drawers, looking through bookshelves and decaying books, and throughout the building for the clandestine documents that were reported to explain the mysterious secrets at Waxley.

But later, after his thesis had been published, he learned that there was a connection with the Schubert painting. Extensive historical research revealed that Ned (and Everett) both had a penchant for Schubert's compositions. And as a result, there was a large oil painting of Schubert hanging on the wall in the back of the administrative office. What David didn't know was that the painting swung open like a door – and was rumored to reveal the purpose behind crematory number seven – which was thought to have some special power.

And David stood in the office, looking at the faded, weathered painting. How such an artistic masterpiece could still be hanging in this office, basically unharmed and untouched for decades was beyond his comprehension.

But he approached it, reached to the right side of the frame, and it slowly opened...

Jacob eased the door open with a creak and his mouth dropped open.

The room was empty but pristine. The light glowed as if the power were still on; the high-polish of the hardwood reflected the grandiose crystal chandeliers. Brilliant green potted palms were nestled in the corners and the paint looked fresh.

There *was* organ music wafting from an unseen player. The room was bathed in soft light; large, standing potted ferns, next to side couches and chairs; small wooden chairs were lined in rows.

And then he heard the voice. A familiar voice from the other side of the room.

"Jacob? Is that you?"

He caught his breath.

He took a few slow steps inside. The carpet in the entryway was flawless, it looked recently shampooed. The edge of the carpet flowed towards the wood, and he was hit with the smell of formaldehyde mixed with the smoky scent of burning incense.

He looked to the left.

Surrounded by the tall palms, and through the rows of wooden chairs was a coffin. A casket lid was propped open against the wall. And his breath quickened when he saw the body laying inside. He paused and turned towards the casket as the organ stopped playing.

He gasped as she sat up and faced him.

"Jacob? Is that *youuuu*?"

His heart pounded as he took a step back. But he couldn't break away. He recognized her.

He watched as she sat up in the casket, easing herself around to look at him, smiling.

There she was. She propped her arms of the edge of the coffin and lifted herself out, easing her right leg over the side, hoisting her bum and then her left leg, and she eased herself down on a small kneeler.

He remembered now. It was the same dress. Flashes of her funeral peppered his mind; as she walked, her body looking just as lifeless as it had when he had last seen it twenty-seven years previously. She staggered through the aisle, jolted heavy footsteps, her arms stretched outwards, her eyelids still sewn shut.

"Oh, Jacob…how I missed playing the *choo-choo with you…*"

He fell against the wall and dropped the flashlight as the room went dark. The organ stopped playing; the chairs were gone; there was no longer the scent of incense but rather the odor of death and decay.

"Gramma!?" His voice reverberated against the silence. There was no light, save the faded yellow of his flashlight.

Debris was scattered everywhere.

Play the choo-choo...

He bent down and picked up the flashlight and shined it across the room.

No coffin.

No Gramma.

Play the choo-choo with me...

And silence. His breathing quickened. He scanned his flashlight across the room. There were several boarded up windows on the opposite end, and a broken casket on the floor next to a fireplace.

He turned and charged to the hallway as the door slammed and shook its frame.

Play the choo-choo with meeeeeeeee...

He caught his breath and shined the flashlight up towards the ceiling. A chandelier hung from the ceiling as wires snaked out from the rusted base.

With meeeeeeee...

He heard the determined approach footsteps, but couldn't move. Stone cold, leaning against the wall, his heart attempting to break free from his rib cage.

He closed his eyes and focused on his breathing. When he heard a muffled voice. He hoped it was David. He opened his eyes and turned his head. And then, in the dark distance, he saw a flashlight.

"Jacob?"

He felt the pressure in his chest release. "I'm here, David. Where have you been?!"

They rejoined at the entrance to the foyer, holding their flashlights pointed down towards the floor. Jacob saw the outline of David's face against the darkness.

But nothing else.

"I found the secret documents!" he said, holding a stack of yellowed file folders and shining his flashlight on it.

Jacob looked at the files he was waving in the light. He found it hard to believe that everything came down to a pile of yellowed folders. And David...there was something…different…about him. Jacob couldn't put a finger on it. But David seemed a little overly excited about the stack of papers he was waving around.

"Lookie here! All we have to do is find the crematory. All the answers will be *there!*"

Jacob shook his head. "Look back there," he said, shining his flashing light behind him. "I just saw my Grandmother back in the room, and she's been dead for decades. No way, man. This project is done."

David scowled.

"No," David said. "It's *not* done."

Jacob lunged forward and grabbed David's collar. "Yes it *is!* Listen to me! Didn't you hear what I told you?! I just had a vision of my dead grandmother back there! This place is beyond help. Past research. This place is fucked *up!*"

David pried Jacob's fingers from his collar. "Look," he said. "You chose this topic as your thesis. And this is what it is. You chose to come alone tonight, which I told you back on campus was a bad idea. When you wander around alone in this place, it will get inside your mind. But now, this is your topic. So it's time to man up and get to *work*!"

Jacob scoffed and shook his head. He picked his flashlight up from where he had dropped it on the floor.

"I just…wasn't expecting this type of activity. Thought the place was dead."

David turned and pointed towards the opposite side of the hallway. "You have to be careful in this place, Jacob. This is why I said don't go alone. Crematory is down there," he said. "Last door on the right and down the stairs. I'll wait up here."

Jacob turned around. There was something about David that seemed off. "You're kidding, right? You just told me not to explore this place alone. Where are you going?"

David smiled and turned back towards the foyer. "You just have fun exploring, little Jacob…"

As David disappeared around the corner, Jacob called out.

"You going to meet me down in the cremation chambers?"

David's response was a song, and faded off into the background. "Not unless you wanna play the *choo-choo* with me…"

And then the hallway went dark again.

Jacob slapped his flashlight a few times, and it shined down the dank corridor. Amidst the trash and debris, he could just make out a door at the end. There was just a hint of faded moonlight through the musty, broken glass; but it was far ahead.

Far down through the hallway.

And the doors that lined the hallway spoke to him, as if they were saying… *enter me… discover my secrets within…*

He shined the flashlight along the walls. Graffiti peppered the broken plaster, but each door remained intact…and closed.

Still, he chose to forage on.

Because now he knew. It was confirmed. Waxley had a certain power; an indiscriminate penchant for exploring the deepest recesses on one's mind.

His suspicions were confirmed. So he chose to press on. To find the cremation chamber, where he was confident all the answers would be.

David had insisted he go there, in the deepest recesses of the funeral home, down into the basement, where the bodies would have been.

Where they would have been prepared, and embalmed, and cremated.

As he moved forward, his feet shuffled along the floor as he held the flashlight downwards, navigating the hazards.

But it wasn't the hazards, nor was it the darkness, the solitude, or the question of where David had disappeared to again. For the flashlight offered a cut through the dark void; a life preserver in a sea of uncertainty.

The only other light, the fading daylight at the end of the lengthy hallway, all the way at the end, which seemed so incredibly far away at that particular moment, was rapidly dissipating.

And even as he shuffled down the hallway, even as he ventured deeper into Waxley, as he looked at the oak frames of the doors as he passed them, still intact, he could feel the hallway speaking to him…in a presence that he had not felt earlier.

One which he could not describe.

But of a feeling.

Of being watched. But not by a person. Or an animal.

But he was being watched.

He caught his breath and focused on the door at the end of the hallway. He reached his free hand up to help steady the flashlight as the silence penetrated him.

He closed his eyes, as he felt a breeze against his face, blowing in from the cracked window.

There's no solitude quite like the darkness of the coffin…

In his mind, he saw the photo of Ned, standing in front of the Mortuary building.

No solitude like the darkness of a coffin, Jacob.

He caught his breath and turned around, shining his flashlight through the hallway. The light didn't go far. He saw a rat scurry across the floor through trash and broken glass.

"Is someone here?"

His voice reverberated against the dark silence. He only half expected David, who seemed lost in his research, to answer. He was apparently oblivious to what Jacob was experiencing.

"Ned?"

Could Ned still be here? Wandering the halls of Waxley?

And then the wind stopped blowing, ushering a new layer of silence.

But Jacob kept his eyes closed, listening to the silence of the hallway. As he strained to listen, he discovered that while the hallway appeared dead, that the outdoors was far from silent. He could just make out the cicadas outside in their understated song.

And as he listened to their music, there was a likening to a chorus, to the strings he would play in the Orchestra back on campus; like a score of violins, playing a long, single, solitary note, in unison, but then, there was the music of violins.

Of the cellos, clarinets and flutes…

It wafted through the hallways from the administrative offices near the foyer; playing, on the phonograph; as the hallway doors, which were closed, were no longer decrepit.

The wood had just been fresh painted.

The floor was spotless and the walls were clean.

Waxley was the premiere Funeral Home in the area, and despite the recession, there were those, particularly whose fortunes had remained intact after the crash, still opted for Waxley's opulence.

Electric candelabras lined the lengthy hallway, nestled between the wooden doors, leading down towards the door which led outside.

Rosa was in the foyer, standing on a velvet side chair dusting the lowest tier of the hanging crystal chandelier.

"Ned!" she called out.

And then the music stopped.

The office door opened and Ned emerged, putting his jacket on. "Yes?"

"I cannot reach the top," she said, easing herself down from the chair. She dragged it across the black and white marble floor and centered it underneath the hanging mirror.

"That's fine, Rosa. You're heading home soon, I gather?"

She looked up at Ned and nodded. "Yes, sir." She opened a small closet on the opposite wall from the mirror, and placed her small feather duster on a shelf inside. She looked up at Ned and nodded and she closed the closet door softly. As she opened the large entry doors, stepping out into the brilliant sunshine, Ned could feel the waft of humid air hit him. But he walked out onto the large porch.

The Waxley Funeral Home sat abandoned on the terminus of Route 27 in the western side of

Miami – past the stately mansions and palm tree lined avenues of Coral Gables; the only access to the mortuary had been a small, two lane road under a shaded oak canopy, which was dark and shaded even on the brightest and hottest of Florida summer days.

Very rarely had there been traffic on Ascension other than funeral processions. Hearses were a common occurrence on the tiny road, leading somber processions towards Resurrection Cemetery, linked to the mausoleums connected to Waxley.

As Rosa walked through the gardens and down to the large wrought-iron gate, Ned's attention turned to the cemetery through the patch of trees. As he looked at the stone markers rising upwards from the ground, he thought of Mr. Waxley's letter.

I am certain you will guard the legacy of Waxley with your life…

He looked out towards the front gate.

Rosa was gone.

Probably half way down Ascension now, almost at the bus stop.

He doubted Rosa knew.

She couldn't know.

There were footsteps creaking on the second floor.

Jacob snapped his head upwards and shined the flashlight up towards the ceiling, his breathing short and rapid; his heart beating through his chest. He took a breath in and held it for a moment.

It could be David.

Yes, David probably went upstairs when he was exploring the hallway. That had to be it.

He exhaled.

His thoughts brought a sense of relief, if only for a moment. He heard the footsteps right above where he stood, his feet planted on the hardwood. Was David standing right above him?

It had to have been.

He thought of Gramma in the room at the other end of the hallway. Lying in her casket in the rose tinted lighting. And the organ music playing. But that wasn't real. That was just his mind playing tricks on him...wasn't it?

And he thought shouting up towards the ceiling might not be a good idea.

"Mind's playing tricks on you."

His voice, soft, gravelly, sounded louder than he intended it to be against the otherwise silent, dark hallway.

But was the pounding in his chest a result of an overactive imagination?

He spun the flashlight over towards the door.

A scratched brass sign had CREMATORIUM: EMPLOYEES ONLY engraved on the front.

A spider crawled across the door as he heard the footsteps again, this time moving away from him.

His mouth dropped open.

He had forgotten that David – or was it David – was standing right above him the entire time. And now David, or whatever it was, moved further away. Jacob had no inkling as to what the floorplan was upstairs. But certainly it was just he and David in the Mortuary, right?

Come see my death box...

He covered his mouth.

His eyes darted around the corridor...

For Jacob's mind was playing tricks on him.

Wasn't it?

And as the footsteps started to descend the staircase, slowly, methodically, heavy shoes clobbing on hardwood, he caught his breath.

"David?" He spoke softly, shining his flashlight towards the center of the hallway. But the light wasn't powerful enough; it couldn't penetrate through the expansive archway into the foyer; and the sunlight had faded to complete darkness.

He called out a little louder. "David...is that you?"

But there was no answer.

The footsteps continued.

A thud with each wooden stair; the shoes – or perhaps the boots – were certainly heavy. Jacob closed his eyes, trying to picture David. When they were standing outside, by his truck. What shoes was David wearing? Sneakers, he thought.

Not heavy work boots.

And then the footsteps reached the bottom.

There was a shuffle. As if a foot were being dragged.

"David…are you hurt?"

But the drag and shuffle continued, getting closer, until there was movement; just at the point where his light faded, at the tiny crest of golden hue, there was a glimpse, a subtle movement of an arm in the fading light.

And then Jacob turned to the door.

He grasped the handle.

It was raspy and grating, rusty feeling. But it turned.

But the door wouldn't budge.

And the sliding continued.

Coming closer as his breathing became more urgent and louder. He shoved the flashlight into his jeans pocket and threw his body against the door. Nothing.

The sliding was closer. Probably past the second door by now.

He took a step back and charged against the door. The frame shook as it tore from its hinges and he crashed into darkness.

The sliding continued, further and closer, and he jumped to his feet. He pulled out his flashlight and snapped it back on. It appeared to be a receiving room of some sort. Tile flooring. Stark walls. Lined with stainless steel countertops.

But there was a single door in the corner, and he headed forward. No time to think. He reached out for the handle, and it turned with ease. The door creaked open as he heard the shuffling behind him.

He turned and shined his flashlight down a set of wooden stairs. He knew where that led to.

There would be a large freight elevator on the other side most likely.

For coffins.

And then, the hallway door behind him creaked open wider. He caught his breath in his throat. It couldn't be David. He turned his head slowly as his heart thumped heavily in his chest. He saw the glimpse of the edge of the door…a towering dark shadow…

…and tore down the stairs, taking two steps at a time. Fallen trees blocked what looked like a large sliding door. There was no time to try to excavate. The shadow upstairs *clearly* wasn't David. And Jacob wasn't going to stay and find out.

His truck was outside.

But there appeared to be no access from this lower level. And the only way ahead appeared to be a long, dark hallway…hopefully there was a door at other end.

He navigated the fallen debris; a damaged wooden coffin lay on its side blocking the entrance. He held the flashlight in the crook of his arm as he climbed up on the coffin. He winced as his foot tore through the lid, the wood shattering.

Oh God…

He stepped on something soft.

Please don't be a body…please don't be a body…

The ceiling shook as dirt rained down through the rafters. There was no time to think about a corpse in the coffin. He tossed the flashlight in the hallway before him. It landed haphazardly and shined against rubbish and debris; it's light shining against the ceramic tiles on the wall.

Jacob spilled over the side of the coffin and into the hallway, nearly slicing his face on a pane of broken glass which jutted from the first door.

The floor above shook again.

The rafters creaked.

"That floor may not hold up," he said to himself.

He turned and picked up his flashlight. There were scattered wooden folding chairs, trash and broken glass throughout the hallway, but he backed slowly, deeper into the dark recesses, turning frequently and shining the flashlight ahead to navigate the litter of debris.

But held his focus on the receiving room ahead. And as he was approaching the final door, he saw a faded and chipped "7" painted on the last door.

He snapped his head towards a crash.

The rafters spilled down from the floor above with a shower of dirt, cement and drywall. His mouth dropped open.

He was trapped.

He shook his head and muttered to himself. "The entire fucking *floor* just caved in…"

He shook his head and shined his flashlight.

There were floor beams spilling down to the lower level at an angle. He saw an old, tattered couch, flooring and wood. All blocking his way out.

Unless there truly was a way out if he went further in.

He turned and shined his flashlight against the door again.

Number seven.

He shined the sphere of light along the dirty, blood scraped walls. And then he knew. His mouth dropped open as he realized what this hallway had been used for: these were the cremation chamber rooms.

And he was standing before chamber number seven, the chamber he was looking for! He felt his fear wash away, and he remembered watching an old documentary about Waxley that aired on the Entertainment Focus channel. Yes, that was it!

He shined his flashlight back on the faded door. It was clearly there. That was an unmistakable "7" painted on the door. It was faded, almost completely gone and covered in dirt, but it was still there.

"Ah-ha! So there you are!"

He reached out and grabbed the handle. He tried to turn it. Of course it was locked. He backed up and kicked it with his shoe, but the door didn't budge.

He stood back again. This time he set the flashlight on the floor again.

He slammed his foot against the door and it flung inwards with a crash.

He stood in the hallway, looking inside at the darkness. He could see the glimpse of the edge of the crematorium, reflected by the light that filtered in from the floor.

This was it.

He was breathing heavy but he reached down for his flashlight and proceeded.

He trudged through the debris, tossing aside broken wood boards and trash.

But he was inside.

Cremation chamber number seven.

He looked at the behemoth.

So many bodies must have been burned to ashes in that giant contraption. It was made of brick, but the round door appeared to be of wrought-iron. It was black, surprisingly clean; a pristine death oven.

Burn with me.

His eyes were transfixed on the crematorium.

This was it.

The big mystery that surrounded the scandal of Waxley. And he was right there standing in front of it.

The door slammed.

He didn't react.

His eyes remained on the prize; on the behemoth brick oven. On the round wrought-iron door; massive; like a giant laundry dryer…but not for the same purpose. Not so clinical. So cleansing. But maybe it could be. Cleansing.

His mind was racing.

The cleansing of burning.

Could it be the cleansing he was seeking?

Could he open that door…climb inside…and clear his conscience? Rid himself of his misdeeds? Leave this world behind?

There wasn't a question.

Burn me.

He dropped the flashlight.

All he saw was the latch on the side of the black wrought-iron door. Nothing else existed.

There wasn't Gramma, there wasn't Susan or Darryl or David. This was the do-all, end-all. He saw that latch. And that was it.

Enter me, fill me with your ashes...

He reached up and pulled the door open with a deep groan. He peered inside; it was only darkness. And cold.

All he saw was where he needed to go. Nothing else. "I'm coming," he said, as he climbed in the gigantic cylinder.

Close the door.

"Yes, I will," he said. "I will close it."

In the confines of the crematorium, he reached around behind his back and closed the door with a deep, bass-filled thud.

Cleanse me.

David ran out the front steps of the Mortuary. Their phones would be in the truck. He was certain of that. He had to contact Susan and Darryl.

He stumbled through the overgrown gardens and saw the truck parked at the edge of Ascension. He slipped through the large gates and reached the truck.

He tried the door.

He cursed.

Of course it was locked. He should have known better. Jacob would have the keys, naturally. And of course he stored his backpack in the front passenger seat. He could see it sitting there, staring at him, as if teasing him.

Jacob, though, could be injured or trapped. He had to contact Susan and Darryl. But Jacob had the keys to the truck. He looked inside, at his backpack, sitting on the passenger seat. Just a thin layer of glass separated him and communication. Should he break the glass?

Even if he chose to break the window, he needed to find something to protect his arm. The last thing he needed was to have millions of tiny shards of glass lodged in his arm and hand. He looked around. The sidewalk was lit by a lonely looking public streetlamp which cast an orange glow on the area.

Resurrection Cemetery was nearly pitch black; he doubted there would be anything in there. He scanned the sidewalk. Maybe there would be a lonely, dirty old t-shirt he could use?

But no luck.

And then it hit him.

He peeled off his shirt, and noticed the cool, night air against his bare chest as he wrapped it around his right arm, covering his entire hand.

He clenched his fist, and punched the window. Glass shattered and rained on the street.

He reached inside and yanked the zipper open, fishing around inside through Jacob's notebooks and found his phone.

Susan sat at the research table in the lower level of the university library. The sun had already set; and there were only a small handful of students in the library that evening. As she sat at the center table, researching old newspaper articles on the microfiche machine, Darryl stood at a nearby photo copier feeding it dimes and copying pages from the Journal of American Morticians.

When her phone vibrated on the wooden table.

She was staring at a microfilm reader, and first ignored the vibrating phone. She muttered to herself and shook her head, reading the headline:

Disappearance of Local Mortician Ned McCracken Remains a Mystery.

Darryl returned with a stack of papers. "Hey, your phone's going off."

Susan nodded, but kept her face shielded by the massive machine. "Yeah I know."

And then the phone vibrated against the wood table again. She let out an exasperated sigh and reached under some papers. She picked it up and her face crinkled. "Who is this?"

She pressed the answer button and held it up to her ear. "Hello?" She looked over at Darryl who took a seat next to her. He looked over at her, leaning forward.

Susan rose from her chair. "Start packing up our things. I need to run outside for a minute so I can talk at a normal volume." And she scurried out through the stacks.

She ran through the doors into the windy evening air as the doors slid closed behind her. She talked much louder now. "Ok, Professor Howell. Slow down. What is going on?"

"We're at the Mortuary and Jacob is trapped!"

Her mouth dropped open. "So you guys actually went!? I thought you warned us not to?!"

David's words were short and rapid.

He sounded out of breath. "Yes, Susan. I know. But I approached Jacob later because I didn't want him to go alone. And I had some of my own questions that I was looking to answer anyway. But now he's gone missing. And a large section of the flooring collapsed...and I think he is trapped on the other side!"

"Slow, David. Slower. Do you need me to call the police?"

"No!" David said. "We can't get them involved. This wasn't a University sponsored trip. I could lose my tenure! We were trespassing! No police. Just come."

The library doors slid open and Darryl emerged with a confused look on his face. Susan spun around and he handed her some of the books and her backpack. She cradled the phone in her ear and looked over at Darryl.

"Just come to my car. We have to go to Waxley. I'll explain along the way."

The news of what happened at Waxley in the past was now long gone, but the case remained open in the Miami PD files. After Ned disappeared, suddenly and without warning, the Waxley Funeral Home ceased operation. Now, as Susan and Darryl piled into her small late-model Honda, they were looking for a new person…it was no longer Ned…now it was Jacob.

"Hopefully he'll be okay," Susan said as the engine of her Honda roared to life. She sped out of the parking lot with one destination in her mind.

Waxley Mortuary and Funeral Home.

David saw a set of dim headlights approaching through the darkness. It could only be them. This road was otherwise deserted.

The small sedan pulled behind Jacob's truck with a slight squeak of the brakes. The engine was cut and the lights went off. As David's eyes adjusted, he saw the driver's side door fling open. Susan stepped out. She approached him. "What's wrong with Jacob, Professor Howell?"

"Just call me David here. We're not on campus."

She nodded. "What's going on?"

Darryl slammed his door and joined them as David continued. "He was exploring the cremation chambers...the lower level. There's a hearse pad out back, but from the inside it's only accessible from a set of stairs or a coffin elevator."

Darryl looked over at the dark building, just scarcely visible from the orange streetlamp glow through the trees. "Okay...so we can get in that way?"

David starting walking towards the gates. "No, I think we'll have to go around back. Let's just go. I don't think he's injured...just trapped."

They ran towards the woods as David pulled up front. He stopped in front of a thrush of overgrown trees and pulled the branches apart. "It gets messy in here. And watch for debris. Broken glass, old pipes. Lots of stuff here that could send you to the hospital."

Susan and Darryl both nodded as they eased themselves through the patch of forest.

The Waxley Mortuary was a large, rectangular brick building. There was a small front yard surrounding the property, which led to a thick forest, which concealed the structure from Ascension Avenue. It was nestled in a private corner of the woods.

"We had waited until dusk to gather," David said, as they traversed a large corner of the building. "It shouldn't be much further. Just on the far side over there. Follow that driveway." David shined his flashlight along broken concrete. The driveway surrounded the building, from close to where they had entered, around Resurrection Cemetery on the front side of the Mortuary, and around towards the back where they were steadily approaching.

"This is where the hearses would load the bodies in and out," he said, as Susan and Darryl approached.

They stopped in front of a massive sliding door on the rear side of the building. The cracked pavement opened to a large cemented area...surrounded by overgrown shrubs.

A concealed parking lot.

Plenty of room for a hearse to turn around effortlessly; even if a coroner's van were parked there was well.

The sliding door was closed, and intact.

"There's a smaller entrance door on the side," David said. The others followed as David threw his weight against the door. "I tried this earlier. Tough to open. Probably swelled in the frame over the years."

"It's amazing it's still intact," Darryl said. "Termites didn't infest the building?"

"Oh they did," David said, as the door opened and he spilled into the dark receiving room. "Look inside."

He pointed the flashlight in towards the darkness.

Massive wooden columns reached down towards the cement floor as tiles and insulation hung haphazardly.

"The floor dropped out," David said. "It crashed down earlier."

Susan pulled David's shoulder and spun him around to face her. "Where's Jacob?" Her voice had an edge to it. Darryl attempted to move some of the floorboards that hung from the collapsed ceiling as he called Jacob's name, to no answer.

"He was on this level when the floor collapsed," David said. He looked over at Darryl. "I've already looked for him. I didn't find him. Nothing. But I *know* what he was looking *for*."

Susan crossed her arms and stared at David. "And what was that?"

David took a deep breath and looked around the room. A rat scurried through trash, and disappeared behind a Styrofoam cup. "Crematory number seven," he said, slowly exhaling. Susan looked over at him, and followed his arm. The flashlight shined through the collapsed floor debris. The hallway, which ran deeper into the basement, was partially revealed through the haphazard floorboards.

Darryl leaned inwards and looked through an opening. "Going to take a while to move this," he said. "If more doesn't collapse on us and send us to the hospital...or worse."

David scoffed as Susan gasped.

"Jacob!" she called.

Her voice reverberated against the silence. "Jacob! We are coming to get you! Sit tight!"

There was a rumble from above.

David grabbed Susan and pulled her back. "Come on Darryl!" he said. "It's happening again!"

Dirt rained from above, as they saw a giant crack forming in what was left of the ceiling. They tore outside and onto the broken pavement, as the ceiling caved in, blocking the entrance.

Darryl charged towards David and reached his arm around his throat, pulling him down. He pinned him to the ground. "Where is he?!"

"Darryl! Stop!" Susan said. He pulled back. David sat up and held his throat. He glared at Darryl and looked over at Susan. "I know you guys care for him deeply," he said.

"We all grew up together," Darryl said, folding his arms, looking down at David. "So where is he?"

David shook his head, and sat up, he knees raised in front of him. "My guess is crematory number seven," he said. He looked back up at Darryl and Susan. "And you both have to understand. There's power there. Physically...he's most likely fine. But you can tear all that debris away and climb back there.

But you won't find him. He won't answer when you call him."

Susan lunged down and got directly next to David's face. "So where *is* he then?!"

David eased himself to his feet as Susan matched his moves.

She dug into David with her glare. David looked over at Darryl, whose arms still crossed. Darryl's arms looked beefy, musclebound. He took a step forward.

"Look guys," David said. "We have no time for fighting. Let me remind you that Jacob wanted to come here. He was insistent. The *only* reason I came was so he didn't come alone. And I know what this place is about. But when he was here, he broke away from me and explored on his own. He was aware of the risks. And what we need now is not an excavation through all that debris. Fighting won't get us anywhere."

"And what do we need?" Susan asked, glaring at David.

Darryl unfolded his arms. "So do you have an idea where he could be? How we can get to him?"

David bit his lip and shook his head. "I don't think it's a where...I think it's a *when.*"

DEMONS
OF
MY
DREAMS

THERE WAS A LARGE, ORNATE WOOD FRAMED MIRROR that hung majestically in the receiving foyer of Waxley Funeral Home and Mortuary.

Shortly after the building was built in the early twentieth century, and before the business opened and received its first guest – Everett Waxley had always insisted on calling the customers "guests" as he felt it was more compassionate. The mirror was hung in the massive foyer, across from the large, round wooden receiving table.

Many a guest had turned and paused to check on their appearance in that particular large, rectangular mirror. And even decades later, after Waxley had gone out of business, the mirror had still hung, the gold paint on the wood chipped, the glass covered with dust and a large crack, the mirror still hung in the foyer, as if tribute to a bygone era.

When Jacob and David were exploring the wreckage of the old, dilapidated building, Jacob had paused in front of the mirror as well. While his reflection had been marred by dust and dirt, there was a certain image, a pallet of a discerned subject which permeated his mind.

The dust and dirt of his thoughts were cleared, if just for a moment, when he paused and stood before the mirror. Of the times he had forgotten; the days that might have been filed deep within his mind, amidst other thoughts that might have been more important at the time; there were those times that surfaced when he stood in front of the mirror.

It was precisely then that he remembered a small shoe box on a summer day when he was still only a young boy.

"Macaroni looks dead."

Jacob's face fell, and his lips quivered. Darryl reached over and touched the small, hardened orange and white hamster.

Jacob held the shoe box up and looked down at his pet. "Are you sure? He could just be sleeping."

Darryl shook his head. "No. He is cold and hard. No way he's still alive."

Jacob touched his finger to the little hamster.

"He's *cold*. Look. He doesn't even move!"

Darryl set his basketball down in the grass and craned his neck over and looked down. He brought his face close to the rodent and sniffed. "Dude. You're right. He's dead."

He looked up at Darryl and bit his lower lip. "She's gonna kill me, I know it."

Darryl scoffed and pressed on the tiny rodent with his finger. He gasped and pulled it back. "No she's not. It wasn't your fault."

Jacob sniffled, and rubbed his eyes with his fist.

Darryl looked over at him. "I'm sorry man, I know you loved him."

"I know...but it's *my fault!*"

"Come on man!" Darryl said. "No it isn't. This stuff happens."

Jacob shook his head. "No. It really is my fault."

Jacob placed the shoebox on the dirt at the edge of the forest clearing and got down on his knees. He reached inside with one finger and gently poked its back. It already felt cold. Stiff.

Jacob hung his head.

"I can't tell her."

Darryl grabbed his shoulder and turned Jacob to face him. Jacob opened his eyes and looked directly back at him.

"Yes you can," Darryl said. "This stuff happens. Death happens. Why would your mom be so upset that your pet hamster died?"

Jacob shook his head. "Because I could have taken better care of him."

"What are you talking about? You loved that little guy."

Warm tears streamed down Jacob's cheeks. "Yeah…but I killed him. I didn't *mean* to!"

Darryl raised his arms. "Wait, wait, *wait*. What are you talking about Jacob?"

He hung his head down. "I was trying to hang my Madonna poster this morning. I couldn't reach so I stepped up on Macaroni's cage…"

"…And?"

Jacob's lips quivered as looked up at Darryl. "The top caved in. He just got out of his wheel. And the edge hit him. Or I stood on him. I can't *remember*!"

Jacob covered his face with his hands and sobbed.

Darryl reached his arm around him as Jacob leaned his head on Darryl's shoulder.

"Look man," Darryl said softly, "Should you have used his cage for a step stool? No. But you didn't know it was going to collapse. You *loved* him. And you should tell your mom."

But it wasn't the shoe box that bothered Jacob.

It was the death.

The cold and lifeless body.

Just that morning, his hamster had been spinning in his wheel, unbeknownst that it would be lying cold, stiff and lifeless in a shoebox just hours later.

"We have to bury him," Darryl said. "I'll help you dig the hole."

And then Jacob sat on his knees, placed the small shoe box on the ground, he turned and watched Darryl hop on his feet and walk back towards the garage. He watched him clank and fish through the yard tools and pull out a large, flat shovel. Darryl hoisted it over his shoulder and walked back to the backyard clearing.

There was something about him.

From the day that Darryl approached Jacob, while he had been sitting out in the grass, on the sidelines, as the neighborhood kids played dodge ball, there was a bond.

A connection between the two boys. A friendship that was growing more solid with the passage of time.

And on the day that they were about to bury Jacob's pet hamster, Darryl proved his friendship once again.

Darryl stood over Jacob and tossed the shovel on the ground with a thud. Jacob placed some leaves around Macaroni's body, turned his head, and looked up at Darryl.

He was standing with his hands on his hips.

"That's a pretty big shovel for this little box," Jacob said, returning his attention to preparing Macaroni's final resting box.

Darryl shrugged his shoulders and knelt down next to Jacob. "That's all I could find."

Jacob took the lid and covered the box gently. "There's a small garden shovel on mom's side of the worktable."

Darryl started to get up when Jacob reached out and grabbed his arm, shaking his head. "It's fine, Darryl. Never mind, let's just bury him."

Jacob reached over and hoisted the shovel upwards. Darryl rushed over and took over, plunging it into the soft earth. He stood on the edge, driving it into the ground, and eased out a pile of dirt, placing it on the side. He repeated this a few times, after which there was a small hole. Jacob picked up the box and placed it in. he looked up at Darryl, who was leaning against the shovel.

"What if Macaroni were a dog?"

Darryl shrugged his shoulders. "What do you mean if he were a dog?"

Jacob brushed dirt over the box with his hands.

"I mean, if I had a dog to bury, would you dig the hole for me? Would you help me with that?"

Darryl cocked his head to the side, pulled the shovel from the ground, and walked a few steps. "That's a pretty big hole."

"Yeah. Yeah it is."

Jacob covered the small shoe box with dirt and packed it with his hands and Darryl watched, holding the shovel at his side. Jacob looked up at Darryl. His best friend on the block who had blocked the light that one day years ago when he was watching the other kids on the street play a game of kickball.

Burying a pet together.

That's one of the more somber things that friends do, for certain.

Jacob looked over at Darryl, who stood, leaning on the shovel. "But would you help me dig a bigger grave? Like for a dog?"

"You're worrying me, Jacob."

Jacob shook his head. "I'm just asking you. If I ever had a dog one day, and that dog were to die, would you help me dig a grave that big?"

Darryl stood straight and picked the shovel up from the ground. "You know the answer to that. For now, just take better care of your animals."

Jacob looked down at Macaroni's grave and sighed.

"Yeah. But even if you take perfect care of them, one day…they will die."

Darryl leaned on the shovel, looking down at Jacob. "Yeah they do. And yes…if you ever had a dog…and that dog died…of course I would help you."

Jacob raised his eyes and looked up at Darryl. "Even if we were eighty years old?"

Darryl shook his head and cracked a smile. "You really are looking into the future, aren't you?"

Jacob rose to his feet, still looking up and raised his eyebrows.

Darryl slung the shovel over his shoulder. He extended his arm and Jacob leaned into his friend's shoulder. As they walked towards the garage, Darryl nodded. "Yeah. Of course I would dude. Even if we're eighty. We're on this roller coaster together."

Jacob's head was throbbing.

He kept his eyes closed.

There was an impenetrable silence to his room. He flung the sheets from his body, treasuring the cool air against his sweaty skin. He opened his eyes and looked up at the ceiling. A small spider scurried out of the crack that ran across the length of the ceiling.

He turned over and swung his legs onto the cold linoleum. On a small, wooden bedside table, on top of his brown leather journal, was his small, gold pocket watch. He picked it up, held it in his palm, and rubbed his eyes with his free hand. He reached down and opened it.

His eyes widened and he gasped.

He flung the watch on the bed and ran to the small closet. No time for a bath this morning. He was already running late. Mr. Waxley would not be pleased.

He pulled out his brown suit – which was actually two different shades of brown which he hoped wouldn't be noticed – and fished his matching fedora from the high shelf. He lay the pants on the bed next to the jacket. He could feel the warm air blowing in from the open window.

He pulled off his white sleeveless shirt and tossed it on a small, steel chair in the corner and headed into the bathroom. He turned the hot water faucet with an audible squeak, and the water started flowing in to the ceramic basin. He pulled a small, white wash cloth from the wall cabinet, and ran it under the water, pulling back and wincing.

He turned the right faucet and held his hand under the water, waiting for it to adjust. He reached up and smeared his hand across the mirror, clearing the steam.

And his eyes widened.

A flash ran through his mind – just for a moment. He looked out into the tiny studio with the steel frame bed and the mattress with the spring that stuck out the side. He ran to the window, hoisted it up, and stuck his head out. The same usual activity. The cobblestone street below. He saw a new model Cadillac driving behind a horse-drawn carriage. Sign of the times. The automobile, they called it. The same dusty sidewalk with the newspaper stand, the men in their suits despite the heat, checking their pocket watches, and the ladies carrying their umbrellas, in their long, summery dresses and tiny waists, shielding themselves from the shimmer of the sun.

He ran to the bed and opened his pocket watch again. "No!"

He ran back to the bathroom and washed under his arms.

It was the same, warm, humid Miami air that he always knew. The same little room. The same view from outside his small window. The hum of activity. Even the motorcars that were starting to populate the streets these days.

But the Great Depression was in full force.

Just as close as were the Duesenbergs and Cadillac town cars, there were others standing in line for a single loaf of bread, handed out in a brown paper bag, on the sidewalk below his single room. And when he turned and looked back at the bed, he hoped that Waxley would not notice his patchwork of clothes.

He remembered seeing the advertisement when he had picked up a copy of the Herald.

There it was. Almost perfectly circled with the ring from a coffee cup. Found on the streets, blowing towards him as he walked past the bread line. As if it were meant to be:

HELP WANTED

Apprentice needed for the Waxley Mortuary and Funeral Home. Please apply in person.

The newspaper blew down the sidewalk as Jacob headed down Ponce de Leon on a January morning when a rare cold front was coming through Miami. He saw it ahead. The wind carried it as it soared several feet into the air, and then it rested on the sidewalk once again. Those who stood in the bread line were oblivious to its presence; but Jacob was focused on the blowing newspaper. There was something about it that he found mesmerizing; it was certainly a sign of the times. Coral Gables was the more affluent area of town, or so he had once thought.

But since the crash, even Coral Gables was not immune to blowing trash and bread lines.

The newspaper was caught by another gust of wind, as it soared towards him, landing against his legs. He stopped and reached down.

He grasped the thin pages with his fingers.

There it was.

He knew that he had to get a job.

But jobs were scarce, if any. The bread line that he stood next to wrapped around the next block. But there…in the Herald…on that blustery January morning…was a job in the classifieds. The coffee ring circled it; brought it right to his attention if that job were meant for him, and only him.

As he read the advertisement, his eyes widened.

He then knew had to find some clothes. Something as professional as he could find. And he knew there was a dumpster at the end of the street. He folded and tucked the newspaper under his arm, and headed forward with a spring in his step.

As he stood later in his small rented room, he laid his found clothes out on his small wire framed bed.

The wide-lapel jacket was fashionable, but, of course, found in a dumpster in Coral Gables. It looked like it was once quite elegant. There was a small tear in the right lapel. Otherwise, it seemed fine. Jacob didn't understand why someone would discard a seemingly wearable jacket when everything was so scarce, but he considered it a lucky find.

After he showered, he pulled on a pair of wide tall pants, rising up above his navel. He snapped on his suspenders over his shirt, and looked at himself in the mirror. He combed his hair back, slicked. He smoothed his hair on the sides and nodded. Not exactly a tailored suit, but this would have to do.

As he left, he had a swing in his step, and tipped his hat at a passing lady in the hallway before swinging open the elevator cage.

The dumpsters were a gold mine.

The street scene was like an old silent film.

As Jacob walked down the sidewalk, and headed towards the bus route, his mind was penetrated by the death fascination. He knew it as a child. His memories, though, were benign.

And also unexplained.

While he didn't question their validity, his determination that the memories were somehow fabricated seemed like a farce. There was something different about that morning.

He closed his eyes for a moment as he stood at the corner, standing on the edge of the sidewalk waiting for a carriage to pass. There was nothing else. He lowered his head and pinched the crest of his nose, and shook his head. The bed was the same. It was the same dirty old mattress, with the same rogue spring that had pierced the fabric and jutted into his back.

Everything was truly the same.

But why did things seem so...different?

And he couldn't put a handle on it.

He clearly remembered searching for work.

But why was the newspaper so precisely timed to flop against his shins on his morning walk through the bread lines?

He opened his eyes, looked up and saw the bus pull up in front of him. He brushed the thoughts off as the door swung open. The driver tipped his cap, nodded and smiled, as

Jacob grabbed the wooden railing and climbed up the steps. He started walking through rows. The bus was crowded. As he passed several rows, he felt a hand grab his forearm. He looked down at a heavyset man in a three piece suit.

He looked at the man.

His big, bushy mustache was trimmed and neat. But there was something unusual about him. And when the man released his grip on Jacob's arm, he looked towards the back.

And then up front.

And then he grabbed the wooden pole that separated the two sections of the bus.

His face shifted as he wrapped his fingers around the wood. The bus accelerated and he caught his feet for a moment. He turned around once again and looked at all the people sitting in the back of the bus.

Something wasn't right.

That he knew.

But he couldn't put a finger on it.

As he looked out the window and saw the passing cars stop for carriages, he saw another line for food. The people stood, their clothes tattered, their mouths open, holding wailing children, chatting among one another, waiting for the soup that was being handed out in bowls at the beginning of the line.

Something most certainly wasn't right today.

The bus pulled onto Ascension, and as he stepped down the stairs and thanked the driver, those feelings washed away.

He stood in front of the majestic building, looking at its brick and wood construction, as it seemed to peer at him through the thick of the trees.

The wrought iron gates were closed, but a uniformed attendant stood at the side.

On the side, with brass on black iron, nestled in the stone wall:

WAXLEY MORTUARY AND FUNERAL HOME

"Uh, I beg your pardon."

The guard looked up as Jacob held his hand up. The guard nodded.

"I am here for the apprenticeship position," he said. He held up the folded newspaper as the guard peered through the iron bars. "There was an advertisement. In the paper. Are you still hiring?"

Jacob noticed that the guard was smartly dressed in a long, black tuxedo with pronounced lapels and flowing tails. He looked over at Jacob with a discerning look. His forehead crinkled as his eyes pierced Jacob. "Mr. McCracken is tending to a service," the guard said sternly. "But you may proceed to the front doors and Rosa will guide you to the receiving parlor."

Jacob raised his eyebrows and maintained eye contact as the guard reached towards the lever and swung the massive gates inwards. He stepped back, holding on side of the gate. His expression was now solemn, and he watched as Jacob took several cautious steps across the property threshold.

"Sir," he said, and nodded. As Jacob cleared the gates, the guard swung the iron behemoths inwards silently. As he latched the gates, the guard turned as Jacob stood and watched. The guard returned to his small station and turned back towards Jacob. The guard gestured towards the building. Jacob turned quickly, and then back towards the guard. He gestured again towards the building. "Good luck, sir."

And then he returned to the guard house.

Jacob stood in front of the narrow driveway. The giant oak trees shaded the black pavement, as splotches of sun danced across the ground. A light breeze blew through the treetops. Jacob looked ahead; the red brick building sat through the forest, through the manicured shrubbery that lined the path.

There were cars parked through the trees to his right. Luxurious models, he could tell. Long, slender engines; thick whitewalls. Carriages with curtains. And then when he looked further towards the clearing, into Resurrection Cemetery, he saw a glimpse of color. Ladies with hats. Gentlemen with top-hats, suits with long tails, and canes.

He stepped onto the stone path next to the turnaround. The grass on either side was cut short; brilliant green, not a patch of brown; meticulously tended, surrounded by sculpted green bushes, rising from a colorful blanket of garden flowers.

The doors were solid wood; heavy. He found an imposing brass knocker, which reverberated with a deep thud when he knocked. He stood, smoothed his jacket, and waited.

After a few moments, he turned back towards the woods. The cars were still lined up on the turnabout and the ladies and gentlemen were still visible through the trees. No movement, it seemed.

He grasped the cool handle and banged three more thuds against the massive doors. After another moment, the door latched.

He took a deep breath, drawing his jacket together one last time.

The door swung open to darkness.

The woman who opened the door slowly held a feather-duster and wore a black and white maid's uniform. Her brown skin contrasted against the stark white starch in her uniform.

Her black hair was tied behind her head neatly, and framed by a white cap. She smiled warmly.

Jacob cleared his throat. "Um, I am here for the apprenticeship. I saw your ad in the newspaper…"

She nodded and smiled.

She took a step back and swung the door open.

Jacob looked inside. The ceilings soared, and a large crystal chandelier hung above an oversized carved wooden table in the center of a sea of marble. The woman extended her arm towards a set of gleaming, colorful stained glass gates.

"The receiving parlor is that way," she said.

Jacob nodded. "I…was told to see Rosa?"

She nodded. "I am Rosa."

Her voice seemed deep. Mysterious. And despite her position of service, she seemed quite comfortable. Her uniform was pressed; her appearance impeccable…but she projected an aura of confidence that Jacob had not seen with the help. She closed the door behind

Jacob with an audible click. His head spun around.

"Please wait in the room across the foyer," she said, gesturing to the double set of brass and stained glass doors. They definitely appeared to be a gate of some sort. Jacob took several steps closer to the colorful doors. Rosa spun around the center table and glided in front of him, her hand wrapping around the brass handles effortlessly. She leaned slightly towards the door, pulled the long, cylindrical handle downwards, and pulled the massive, swinging door outwards, with a deep groan.

Jacob peered in towards complete darkness.

"Wait in there please."

He turned and looked over at Rosa. She stood, her hands clasped at her waist. Her face was expressionless. "Go on," she said.

He took an uncertain step forward, his shoe crossing the threshold where the light from the foyer ceased. And when inside, she closed the door behind him with an audible *click*!

And then he was alone in silence.

And with his thoughts. The unexplained visions that cascaded through his mind as he stood in that particular room.

The uncertain mystery of his memories – those which seemed real and the others which seemed fabricated. But there he stood; wondering where everything had gone. Why the darkness would wrap around him, its fingers caressing his limbs.

But there was the mirror that he'd noticed when passing through the foyer; the reflection, though, changed when he passed by it. And as he stood in the darkness, waiting for someone to come, waiting for light to penetrate, he thought of the mirror in the foyer.

How the reflection would change.

And the mystery that surrounded it; the feeling that there was something *wrong* with what the mirror reflected, what had flashed before his eyes while following Rosa; how the mirror revealed the fleeting reflection; but the vision was a fallacy, wasn't it?

The foyer clearly was not a dilapidated room filled with trash and broken light fixtures.

But rather a grand foyer filled with marble and stained glass.

Brilliant green ferns; crystal chandeliers and mahogany woodworking.

And as he stood in the darkness, he waited. Thought of the mirror.

And then, he closed his eyes. Why did the mirror reflect such destruction and torment? Such loneliness? Even if just for a fleeting moment?

There was a new thought, something different, which he couldn't place. Something that his mind embraced, but failed to understand, at least not in his current frame of mind.

There was the distinct voice of a woman. And the sound of a little boy, sitting on a stool, softly crying. The tears streamed down his face, wetting his small, round, red cheeks.

"It is not your fault, Jacob."

Her voice was familiar.

"Macaroni is dead…"

The little boy leaned forward, placing his head in the woman's bosom, sobbing. There was a certain familiarity about the scene; the kitchen was warm, inviting, but mysterious beyond a small sliver of light, revealing the scene, the woman comforting a crying boy, in a sea of impenetrable darkness.

"It is not your fault that he died..." she said again, her hand wrapped around his back, holding him closer to her.

And then the scene faded to darkness when he heard a piano start to play softly. Perhaps in a distant room, but he could hear the melody through the darkness.

He gasped as he heard the door creak open. A sliver of light emanated from behind him, but did nothing to penetrate the darkness.

And then the deep, baritone voice of a man jolted him.

"Did you enjoy yourself in here?"

Jacob turned and saw a dark silhouette against the light flowing from the foyer.

He tried to speak but couldn't.

The mysterious figure let out a small chuckle. He remained a silhouette until two lamps on the far end of the room snapped on, bathing the room in soft, incandescent light.

Jacob took a breath as his mouth dropped open. The man appeared to be similar in age to him. Perhaps younger. Dressed similarly, but clearly in a much more expensive suit. And most likely not found in the dumpster on the side of Ponce de Leon.

The piano music sounded louder once the stained glass doors were opened. Jacob looked out towards the foyer and out towards the source of the piano music.

"It's Beethoven's Moonlight Sonata," the man said, gesturing for Jacob to sit.

They sat across from each other in overstuffed side chairs. "Rosa plays it each and every afternoon. You met Rosa, I gather?"

Jacob smiled and nodded, but said nothing.

They sat in an awkward silence until the man extended his hand. "I am Ned. Ned McCracken. I understand you are here to see me?"

Jacob adjusted his posture and cleared his throat. "Yes...I...the apprenticeship..."

"Ah, yes," Ned said. "The Herald ad. And you think you are the right man for the job?"

Jacob nodded. "Yes…I –"

"– you simply need a job or you feel compelled to work here?"

Jacob sat and considered what Ned had said. He'd never considered working at a Funeral Home before. He couldn't even really remember his past. Like he always lived in the present; there was nothing that stood out in his mind from the world he was in. He knew about the bread lines.

And why they were there.

But on the bus, he'd been shocked to discover the segregation. As if he were a stranger in a strange land; yet, somehow the purpose he felt there had been significant; and there, also, was the purpose of finding Waxley.

And speaking with Ned McCracken.

"Working in this position requires much more than a clinical understanding of death," Ned said.

Jacob listened to the music.

Rosa playing the piano, in some seemingly distant, unseen location towards the other side of Waxley. There was something that just seemed different, yet purposeful. As if he were meant to be there, but with no clear understanding of why he was there.

Ned stood, as Jacob raised his eyes and looked up at him. Ned adjusted his jacket and buttoned the top button. "It's a calling," he said, matter-of-factly. "Going into this line of work is not just applying to a job in the classifieds. It's either meant for you…or it's not. I'm not going to try to convince you that you would be a worthy successor to run this operation. It's a choice that you and you alone can make."

Jacob stood as they headed towards the foyer. "How can you determine if I am the correct one to be your successor?"

Ned cocked his head to the side, his mouth in a slight smile.

"Well," he said. "Only your heart can determine what's right. You have to look deep within your soul. Answer the calling if it's there."

Jacob nodded, looking at Ned the entire time. Ned returned the gaze. Jacob thought his eyes looked wide and innocent, but his face projected experience. And presentation. His clothing was impeccable. His hair was slicked and tight.

"Are you thinking about joining us, Mr. Benjamin?"

Ned stood in the foyer as the piano stopped playing. He stood and turned towards Jacob, clasping his hands at his waist. Jacob heard the clap of heels down the winding, marble stairway. Jacob turned his head to see Rosa descending the stairs, her hand gliding on the brass bannister. She was still in uniform, and looked up at Jacob, her mouth still pursed closed but with warm, open eyes. She moved down next to Ned, and stood next to him, clasping her hands at her waist as well. The expression on her face lightened as another set of footsteps approached; heavier, deeper, yet softer. A tall and lanky man approached, wearing a pair of stark white trousers and white doctor's jacket.

There was bright red blood on the gloves he was wearing.

He turned his head and looked over at Jacob and nodded. "Pat," he said, joining the others. He clasped his hands at his waist, staining the jacket.

They each stood and watched Jacob. He stood looking back at each of them, listening to his own breathing, until Ned broke the silence.

"Are you ready to join us?"

Miami Beach. *Present Day.*

CLARISSA GREEN HAD A SMALL tarot card reading operation on the sidewalks of Miami Beach, about thirty minutes by car (without encountering the legendary Miami traffic) from the resting place of Waxley Mortuary. She was a tourist showcase: the front windows were covered in purple curtains, and the neon hand hung in the window, next to the sign FIRST READING FREE.

Nestled between the one-story dusty shops on Washington Avenue, along the dirty sidewalks of South Beach, Clarissa's shop encompassed just enough sidewalk space for her door, and a small picture window where she had hung her sign advertising the first free readings and the neon open palm. Just inches further was a diner, which was busy pretty much all day and throughout the night, but the peak hours were the wee hours of the morning with the late night club goers and tourists, and so Clarissa opted to work mostly at night, when the sidewalks were filled with people in the stifling Miami humidity, the wail of the horns in the chronically congested Washington Avenue traffic, which seemed to reach a crescendo past midnight.

But on that particular day, Clarissa shoved her key into the lock in the morning, when the sun was still peeking over the nearby Atlantic; when the hum of the traffic had temporarily quieted, and the shadows of the nightclubs across the street from the lightening sky seemed to lower the light and temperature.

The light from the diner next door reflected on her face, but once she yanked the door open, she emerged into complete darkness. She could see the small, red blinking light on the reception desk in the tiny waiting room, which instantly caught her attention. She had not seen that light blinking in months.

Who had called?

She rushed over to the machine and flopped her bags on the counter, pressing the play button. She placed her chin on her hands and leaned her elbows on the counter as she listened to what sounded like an uncertain female.

Uh...hello. I actually researched your services on the internet. But we are in need of a medium. I'm Susan Baroni, and a member of a thesis research group with the Nazareth University. We're investigating Waxley Mortuary for our Thesis, however we have a situation where we will require your services. If you could return my call, that would be appreciated.

Clarissa put her pen down and stared at the phone number she had jotted down on the post it note that she hastily grabbed during the woman's short message. She paused for a few minutes, and then looked over at the sliver of light reaching through the slit in the center of the purple curtains.

There was something about the woman's voice.

She certainly sounded young, inexperienced. She had indicated she was a student. And if they were truly investigating Waxley...in over her head.

Once the sun peeked over the buildings across the street and the traffic had increased to its usual activity level, Clarissa called the young woman back and made an appointment with her. Clarissa opted not to bring the woman to her tiny offices, but rather to meet her in a neutral location since this woman was not looking to get a palm or tarot reading, but wanted to hire her for her medium abilities and clairvoyance.

Lester's Diner sat on the edge of Washington Avenue, right next to Clarissa's shop. Clarissa had returned Susan's call promptly. They'd agreed to meet for a cup of coffee that same evening and discuss the situation on their hands.

Susan and Darryl stood at the hostess stand inside the busy diner. The tables were full and it was noisy. The hostess appeared to be a server whose hair was falling out of place as she ran around from table to table, handing out menus and pouring coffee.

She approached Susan and Darryl. She smiled broadly, still holding the coffee pot. "Welcome to Lester's!" She appeared cheerful, despite her messy exterior. Susan nodded and smiled and asked for a booth for four. The hostess nodded enthusiastically, grabbed some menus, and ushered them to the corner booth. Susan looked up as the hostess was about to turn and leave. "The woman who is meeting us should ask for me by name, but won't recognize us when she sees us. So if she asks for Susan or Darryl, would you mind bringing her here?"

She nodded and smiled. "Certainly, darling."

The hostess returned to another group of entering customers as Darryl settled into the booth across from Susan. He picked up his menu and started browsing the selections. Susan followed, and after a few minutes of paging through the heavy, laminated menus, she looked up at Darryl.

He placed his menu down, and looked back at her. He looked pained. "I'm not hungry," he said.

Susan placed her menu down, shook her head and folded her arms. "Me neither."

They ordered coffee and Darryl ordered pancakes as they waited for both Clarissa and David to arrive.

Both were running late, and they could feel the anxiety and tension building as they knew that Jacob needed some sort of help…but were unsure of how to provide it.

Susan's face was shifted with worry. "This Clarissa hopefully will be able to help," Susan said as she stirred some sugar into her coffee. The spoon clanked against the china as she reached for the small, silver creamer pitcher with her free hand. "I mean...I don't know if a *medium* is necessary, but I don't know how else to approach this. We searched the building...and with David's suspicions about that cremation chamber...I don't know what other recourse we have."

Darryl nodded as he took a sip of coffee. "He can't just disappear into thin air." Susan raised her eyes as David approached. He looked like he hadn't slept for days. "But can he?"

"That coffee looks amazing," he added, as he slid in the bench next to Darryl.

Darryl glared at David. "He *can't* just disappear into thin air. Period. Explain that."

David sighed and rubbed his face with his hands, running them through his hair. There was an edge to his voice. "Look, Darryl. I told you about crematory seven. It's not a question of where he is but *when*. That cremation chamber is special. And it has a direct connection to Resurrection Cemetery…and why there are no bodies there."

"Have you slept at all?" Susan asked. She looked at David. His eyes were bloodshot and there were dark bags underneath.

He closed his eyes and shook his head. "Not since before I met Jacob at the mortuary. I've tried to lay down, but as soon as my head hits the pillow, my eyes shoot open."

Susan looked him directly in the eyes. "How weren't you able to stop him?"

The waitress approached and offered David coffee, who accepted and took a big gulp. He looked back at Susan. "There was no stopping him. He was already there when I met him."

She glared at him.

"I went with him so he wouldn't go alone. I *told* him that he shouldn't go alone. And when we got inside…he left and explored on his own."

"So he was on his own anyway then," Susan said, leaning back and lowering her head. She pinched the top of her nose with her finger and thumb. She lowered her hand and looked up.

Susan leaned her head back on the booth as the waitress came over to their table to refill their coffees. Darryl sat in front of a stack of pancakes, holding his small, white coffee cup with both hands wrapped around the base. Susan looked over at him and reached her hand across the table and rubbed his shoulder. David held his coffee cup up as the waitress topped it off with steaming, black coffee. He nodded as the waitress smiled and left, and took a small sip before setting it back on the table.

"Well guys," David said. "It's been…what…twenty four hours now?"

Susan made eye contact with Darryl and they looked over at David. Darryl looked back down at his cup. "Yeah, something like that."

Susan pressed David. "Do you think he's still there somewhere? In some way?"

David raised his eyes and looked at Darryl and Susan. "Let's not get the authorities involved. At least not at this point. We all know this wasn't an authorized trip. I was just going with him to protect him. But he chose to go off alone…"

Darryl banged his fist on the table, as the flatware clanked against china. "Stop *saying* that! How many times are you going to pull that card?!"

Susan jumped. She reached out and touched Darryl's arm, looking at David, and then back to Darryl. "Let's just work to find him," she said.

They all looked up as they heard jingling approach them. A short woman, dressed in a long, flowing sundress, denim jacket, and a multitude of oversized gold and silver jewelry, approached their table.

She smiled and waved. "You must be Susan," she said, leaning forward. She extended her hand towards Susan and used her free hand to move her long, curly auburn hair behind her back.

Her jewelry and trinkets jingled as she moved.

"Clarissa Green," she said, as the hostess returned with a chair. Clarissa slowly sat and eased herself into the booth, smiling brightly with brilliant white teeth, surrounded by bright purple lipstick. She looked at both the men, and then back at Susan. "So this is your research team?" She extended her hand again to David and Darryl, and introductions were made. Clarissa sat at the end of the booth and ordered chamomile tea. She beamed, thanked the server when her tea was placed in front of her, and squeezed a lemon before taking a sip.

She returned her attention to Susan. "So tell me, Susan. Why do you need a medium?"

Susan took a break and cracked a thin, polite smile. "Well..."

David interrupted. "One of our research team members is missing at Waxley."

Clarissa started coughing and set her cup down with a clank. After several minutes and the others' at the table asking if she was okay, she looked over at David with pleading eyes. "Waxley?! What on earth are you going there for?!" She turned over to look at Susan. "I heard your message and thought maybe you were *wanting* to go...not that you'd already been!"

Darryl covered his plate of uneaten pancakes with his napkin, shaking his head. There was a long, exasperated sigh. He looked across the table at Susan. "I told you."

Susan scowled, crossed her arms, and shoved herself back in the booth.

She shot a glance over at Clarissa and shook her head. "*We* didn't go."

David looked over at Clarissa. "You have to understand that Susan and Darryl here are Master's Degree students working on their thesis. This is project research. Jacob, the one who has gone missing, is the project leader."

"And who are you?" she asked. "You're not on the team?"

David looked down at his coffee. "I'm their professor, and —"

Clarissa's mouth dropped open. "You don't even look…"

Susan leaned forward. "I thought we should call the police."

Darryl nodded. "I second that. He's been missing over twenty-four hours."

David raised his hand and looked over at the two students. "Guys. You know we can't do that."

Clarissa closed her eyes and shook her head. She held her teacup with both hands. "This is not a matter for the police," she said. She opened her eyes and sipped her tea again. She made eye contact with each and every one of them. "Do you all know about crematory number seven?" She raised her eyebrows as Susan's mouth dropped open. She looked at David, and their eyes met.

Susan looked back at Clarissa, who sat her cup down softly. She stared back at Susan, and folded her arms on the table.

Susan shook her head slowly. "How did you?"

She smiled softly at Susan. "I know quite a bit about Waxley." Her gaze moved about the table as she spoke. "You all called me because I'm a medium. And what you need to know, is that Waxley has been overrun by spirits since it was built. The hauntings there are nothing new. I've been there."

Darryl chimed in. "So what is with this special cremation chamber?"

He looked over at David. "Number seven?" David nodded and returned his attention to Clarissa.

"It's a portal to the spirit world," she said slowly. "And the spirits flow freely between their world and ours through that chamber." She placed her bag on the table and settled into her chair. "But what you had initially asked me…about conducting a séance…that's not something we can do at Waxley. Too much interference. And with that portal being where it is, the potential for dangerous spirits is very real."

Susan felt a chill run down her spine.

Darryl sat back and folded his arms. "What about Jacob?"

She cocked her head to the side and lowered her eyes. "Well, we can assume that he was somehow…drawn…to number seven. I mean, we don't know for *sure,* but we can proceed with that. It gives us a starting point, and something to work with for locating him."

"So you think he went through there," David said.

She looked at him and nodded. "It's a distinct possibility. There are stories of living people accidentally falling through open spirit portals, and seemingly lost forever."

Susan gasped and covered her mouth.

Clarissa looked directly at Susan. "There are also cases where the people have been located. In some instances, the missing hadn't even gone through the portal at all, and literally were missing."

Darryl unfolded his arms and leaned forward. "And those that went through?"

Clarissa's face fell. "They're usually never seen or heard from again."

Darryl glared at David, who shifted in his seat. He looked at Clarissa. "But what about Jacob? What hope do we have for him if he passed through the portal?"

She sighed. "Well, we can attempt to communicate with him. He could very well be in another time, not even knowing he is out of place. Everything there could seem perfectly normal to him…or just slightly off. But he may not understand why. And he might have memories of *this* world that may not make sense to him there."

"I have a Ouija board," Susan offered.

Clarissa's eyes widened. She shook her head. "Absolutely not," she said. "Too much risk there," she said.

"What type of risk?" Susan asked.

"Waxley is teeming with spirit activity," she said. "Too much risk for evil spirits. There's already a portal. And I can communicate. So leave the board at home."

She set her teacup down as the server placed a small, white ticket on the table and thanked them.

"So," Clarissa said. "I require payment upfront. The best time to go is the present. So I won't accept your cash and suddenly disappear. I work in a fairly short time window. Plus it sounds like this is fairly urgent."

Susan sighed. "Hopefully he will understand the signs we send him."

They arrived at the end of the road where Jacob's truck was still parked next to the rusted gates. David followed in his small blue sedan, with Clarissa riding in the passenger seat. When they pulled forward, Clarissa opened her door and immediately got out of the car.

She approached Jacob's truck as the others joined her. They headed towards the front of the building, and climbed the stairs.

As Clarissa explored the foyer, looking upwards in all directions, Darryl leaned close to Susan. He spoke in a low voice. "Are you sure about this?"

Susan looked at him.

Her face shifted. "What do you mean?"

"Well…people say that these séances can open doors to the spirit world. If there is no door open here, are you sure that's something you would want to open?"

Susan scoffed, looking forward, watching Clarissa glide through the foyer, raising her arms, seemingly dancing in the dilapidated construction, like a fairy.

She raised her eyes back up at Darryl. "Do you honestly think anything is going to happen with this? Look at her. She's a bowl of Froot Loops."

He shrugged his shoulders. "Let's let this play out. I don't really know."

Clarissa stopped in front of the faded, dusty mirror that still hung in the foyer. Her eyes widened as she approached it. She ran her hands along the wood carved edges, as she gasped and her mouth dropped open.

"What is it?" David asked.

She smiled. "There's something about this *mirror*! So much energy coming from it! Like it's alive!" She stared at it, taking several steps back, until she was against the rotted wooden table. She continued her trance, her mouth open. And shook her head. She reached out, running her fingers across the dirtied glass, caressing the frame.

"I feel so much energy from this mirror in particular!"

The reflection was dusty; scratched. It hung haphazardly, their reflections muted in the darkness. But Clarissa stood in awe, titling her head to the side. For she knew.

There was something about the mirror.

She could sense it. This was no ordinary mirror. It was not made of reflective glass...for the reflections...or what they seemed...were not always going to be what they appeared.

She grasped the frame, held it steady against the wall. "I can feel its power run within my body...!"

...Jacob stood in the foyer, just in front of the hanging mirror, and straightened his tie. The smell of fresh paint was in the air, as he turned his head, Ned appeared and placed his hand on his shoulder gently.

He leaned down and smiled. "Are you ready?" he asked. He reached around and helped Jacob get his tie straight. "This is your first viewing, you know." He looked Jacob in the eyes. "You've been here for a while now. Are you nervous?"

Jacob thought about his time thus far at Waxley. And the dark room through the stained glass gates. That first inconclusive night with Ned. But despite the initial uncertainties, Jacob hadn't returned to his tiny little rented room on the fifth floor overlooking Ponce de Leon; for Ned had been warm and inviting. And so had Rosa and Pat. Ned was instantly welcomed as part of the Waxley family.

They treated him like the guest that he was, not just a hired associate. It was a respect that he rather enjoyed. And the learning…about the process of body acquisition, cleansing and preparation, embalming, dressing and casketing all fascinated him.

"This is the trocar," Ned had told him, the very next day, as they donned white surgical jackets and trousers. The harsh light flickered in the lower level embalming room. Ned held up a long, shiny oversized needle. Jacob tilted his head as the reflection from the overhead light caught his eye.

Ned looked over at Jacob.

He held the trocar high so Jacob could examine it; the giant, reflective needle, which Ned turned with his wrist so Jacob could see. Huge, and thick. A wide, piercing mouth, with a sharp point. Jacob shuddered, and looked down, as the body lay on the pr eparation table, covered by a white sheet.

Ned cracked a grin. "You know much about embalming, Jacob?"

He shook his head.

"Well, I can certainly teach you everything."

Ned pulled the sheet away as Mr. Bannister was exposed.

"Now, Mr. Bannister has already been washed. That's the first part of the process." He carefully placed a towel over the man's penis. Ned nodded and Jacob winced as Ned plunged the trocar in the center of the abdomen. Jacob's mouth dropped and eyes widened as Ned looked up, still jamming it into the man's midsection. "The trocar is actually a drainage tool," he explained. "We've set the catheter up on the neck at the carotid artery, there."

Jacob looked up at the glass canisters of bright pink fluid on the counter.

"The fluid is pumped in the body, and the blood drains via the trocar. It's all physics, really."

Jacob's face shifted and he looked at the body.

The mouth was hanging open.

It looked like there were giant bruises throughout his body under his skin.

Ned pressed a button and the process began – a groan of the pump, a whir, and then it started; Jacob watched the pink fluid slowly work its way through the light brown tubing, towards Mr. Bannister's neck.

Jacob leaned over the body, watching Ned adjust the trocar as bright red blood seeped from the wound onto the table. "How long have we been doing this?" he asked.

Ned found a satisfactory spot for the trocar and stood back up straight again. He carefully removed his gloves and shrugged his shoulders. "Embalming, really, has been around since 4000 B.C. – you know, when the ancient Egyptians mummified their dead."

"Uh huh…"

"They believed the mummification – or the embalming – empowered the soul after death. And they believed the soul would return to the body."

Jacob's eyes widened.

Now this had become interesting. "Clearly the process has evolved," Jacob said, watching the overspill of blood accumulate on the table in a small, bright red lake.

Ned leaned over the table, adjusted the trocar, and nodded. "Yes," he said, and cracked a smile. Ned's smile was the same as when he cracked a smile next to him standing in front of the mirror, as Jacob adjusted his tie, preparing to oversee his first viewing.

Ned's teeth gleamed against the fading light of the day's end. "Join me for dinner afterwards."

Jacob looked up, eyes wide, mouth open, as Ned started towards the back hallway.

"You're not coming?"

Ned turned and shook his head. "You're ready, Jacob. You've been here long enough. I have confidence in you."

And then he disappeared around the corner.

Jacob could feel the knot develop in his stomach as he heard a car pull up outside. It was most certainly Mrs. Bannister, arriving early before her scheduled guests.

Jacob looked back over in the mirror and adjusted his tie once again. He reached up and smoothed his hair back. He looked behind his shoulder. Across the foyer, through the massive green fern on the center table, he could see a glimpse of the coffin between the gap in the brilliance of the stained glass gates. He could see Rosa rushing around the room. She had her trademark feather duster. Jacob learned that she always liked to pass through the room one last time just prior to the guests' arrival. She adjusted several chairs that had been lined up in rows facing the coffin; and she spun around and straightened some newspapers on a nearby wooden side table.

And then the door chime rang.

A brass bell, with a chain that disappeared into the wall, hung high above the tall, wooden doors, rang repeatedly, shaking Jacob out of his musing. He saw a silhouette through the frosted glass. The shadow of a large hat clearly indicated that Mrs. Bannister had arrived.

Jacob took a deep breath and smoothed his lapels. He walked to the door, and reached for the cool, brass handle.

And then he paused.

He saw more shadows.

Mrs. Bannister was not alone. There were several more people waiting on the front porch. He saw the dark blotches of moving shadows through the blur of the frosted glass as he cleared his thoughts.

And slowly opened the door.

Mrs. Bannister smiled, her teeth a brilliant white, surrounded by equally bright red lipstick. He thought her reaction was in fact peculiar, given that she was there to bury her husband. He also thought her quite young to have been married to someone so much her senior, but he brushed those thoughts away.

"Do not judge our guests," Ned had instructed him earlier. "Some reactions may seem odd to you. But we all grieve in different ways."

But Mrs. Bannister beamed as she stepped across the threshold, with her entourage of servants. Two butlers dressed in black and white tuxedos followed her, one holding an umbrella over her head, the other holding a large leather bag.

Her lips were pursed and she glared at Jacob. "I had instructed there not to be an embalming. How did this happen?"

She stepped inside and her heavy heels thudded on the marble flooring. The butlers trailed behind her as she approached the stained glass gates. She removed her white glove from her left hand and touched the brass, gently sliding the door open as the casket was revealed, on display at the far end of the parlor.

Jacob quietly rushed to her side.

He leaned close to her ear. "My deepest apologies, Mrs. Bannister. And condolences also. But yes, he was embalmed. Ned phoned you yesterday, correct?"

She nodded and scowled, looking ahead at the casket display. She turned and pierced Jacob with an icy stare. "Then why suggest something like that? A process where he can return if he weren't embalmed? What kind of silly nonsense is that?!"

Jacob placed his hand on her arm and she pulled back. "Where is he, anyway?"

She turned and charged across the foyer, passing the hanging mirror, towards the rear hallway. "Ned!" she called. "Mr. McCracken come here!"

Jacob and the butlers trailed behind her. "Mrs. Bannister, please! He is already preparing a refund for your account. Now please – your guests are to arrive shortly!"

But Mrs. Bannister did not listen.

And she tore down the hallway, all the way towards the end where the small exterior door shined a small amount of light into the dim corridor, and stopped, just in front of the door marked

CREMATORY: MORTUARY
PERSONNEL ONLY

"Mrs. Bannister, *please*!"

She slapped her open palm on the door. "Mr. McCracken! Mr. *McCracken*!" She snapped her head around and waggled her finger at Jacob. Her eyes were piercing and wide. "I expect a *complete* explanation!"

But Jacob wasn't listening to Mrs. Bannister.

He rubbed his arms, noticing the sudden cold in the hallway. The unexplained draft that seemingly came from nowhere. He looked around, saw the flicker of the bulb in the candle sconce on the wall...and opened his mouth to speak...

...Clarissa reached out and touched the broken candle light fixture on the wall, as they stood in the long hallway that spanned the rear side of the building. "Oh yes," she said.

"What is it?" Darryl asked, shoving some trash and debris to the side with his foot. He and Susan looked up at her hand as she caressed the plastic candelabra.

"I sense voices," she said, lowering her head and closing her eyes. She reached out and touched the door, smoothing her hand over the dirty surface. "And this door here…to the lower level…this is what leads to the center of sadness. Of regret. And pain…" She lifted her hand as Susan handed her a tissue. Clarissa wiped her hands as best she could.

They all turned around and looked up as David approached.

His feet shuffled through the dust and dirt. "Cremation chamber number seven," he said, shrugging his shoulders. "That is where everything happens…"

Clarissa nodded and she slowly approached David. "But the cemetery…" she said. "It's in the cemetery where the bodies were…"

Susan placed her hand on Clarissa's back. "Were? What about the bodies, Clarissa? What happened to them?"

She closed her eyes and swallowed hard. And then looked back up at the others. "The bodies…" She turned and looked at the door to the lower level.

CREMATORY: MORTUARY PERSONNEL ONLY

The brass was scratched, the letters faded. But it was still readable.

"There," she said, pointing at the large, closed wooden door. "Through there. I sense it's downstairs. It's calling me. I can hear the voices…"

Darryl moved forward and reached for the handle. He jiggled it and shoved his shoulder against the door. Nothing.

He looked at the others as he took several steps back and then charged the door, raising his leg, crashing his foot against the door. It flew open, slamming against an inner wall.

Clarissa instantly headed through the open doorway. "This is where they delivered the coffins…" she said. She moved deeper into the darkness as her voice trailed off. She stood at the top of the wooden stairs that led downwards, and looked up towards the ceiling.

"I hear music," she said.

The others joined her. Susan looked back towards the front foyer. "I hear it too."

They stopped and listened.

From the front of the building…classical strings…as if a faint, unseen orchestra were playing in the distance.

"That's it!" Clarissa beamed. Her eyes widened as she danced in circles. "I know this piece!"

"It's Schubert," David said, approaching the door, looking back down the hallway. "It's faint. But I recognize it as well."

"Where's it coming from?" Darryl asked.

Susan shook her head. "I don't care. I don't wanna know."

Clarissa laughed. "They are speaking with us!" She took a deep breath, and leaned her head back, closing her eyes. "Oh…*Ave Maria*. I can hear it playing! So soft! So faint! But there…"

Susan's mouth dropped open. "You think...?"

David shook his head and looked over at Susan. "I don't know for certain...but...I do think there is some communication going on here."

After the Bannister viewing had concluded and Ned had consoled the new widow, Jacob approached the front office.

He could hear Schubert's *Ave Maria* playing softly through the closed door, and he knew that Ned would be sitting at the desk, enjoying his afternoon cup of coffee, and reviewing the following day's itinerary.

He knocked softly.

After a short pause, he heard the creak of the desk chair, and footsteps. The door swung open, and Ned stood, his collar loosened, his tie off. His black hair was slightly mussed. Certainly uncommon for him. His eyes were wide, but friendly. After a moment, he raised his eyebrows.

"Can I come in?"

Ned stepped aside and extended his arm. "Certainly. Come in."

Jacob entered and pulled the side chair further away from the desk.

He sat, his arms on the side, his hands in his lap. He watched Ned as he returned to the rear of the desk, to the record player on the far shelf. He lifted the needle and placed it back on the edge of the black disk.

The soft piano and violin filled the room as Ned made eye contact with Jacob, and then returned to his desk. He sat, leaned back, and watched Jacob for a few minutes, until Ned broke the silence.

"Do you listen to Schubert, Jacob?"

He stammered. "Uh, I, ah, sure. Well, yeah, I mean…I guess so."

"Did you know that Schubert only lived to be thirty-two?"

Jacob shook his head slowly.

319

Ned nodded, watching Jacob. His voice was soft; Jacob had to lean forward to hear him over the music. "In that short time he created a fantastic musical legacy," Ned said.

"That he did."

Ned cracked a grin, never taking his eyes off of Jacob. He took a breath, relaxing back in his chair, and placed his arms behind his head. "I know all about you, Jacob. But I do have a question. Are you one of those who has created a fantastic legacy?"

Jacob shifted in his chair and raised his eyebrows. "I would certainly hope so."

Ned nodded and took a sip of his coffee. "Indeed. But you didn't come into my office to discuss a future as a mortician, which I am sure of."

"You read me well, Ned."

Ned cracked another grin. "Well, we've been working next to each other for a while now. But I must confess. I knew you were going to show up here even before you came. You weren't a surprise to me, Jacob. You were scheduled to arrive, just as the others were."

"The others?"

"All of the others who pass through the Waxley Funeral Home and Mortuary."

Jacob nodded, grasped the arms of the chair, shifted his body weight further back, and looked up at Ned. "What is this place, Ned? What is this *time*?"

Ned lowered his arms and nodded. "Your line of questioning is pretty typical."

He stood and walked to the side of the desk, and leaned on the edge, looking down at Jacob, never breaking his eye contact.

"Waxley is more than a mortuary. Think of it more as a...stopping point. For those like you."

"Those like me?"

Ned nodded.

"Yes," he said. "Those who have experienced this period for the first time."

Jacob nodded. "That's what I came here to talk to you about."

"Go on."

Jacob rose from his chair, walked over to the opposite wall, and on the wooden shelves was a silver pot. He reached for a small, china cup and poured himself a cup of steaming coffee. He turned and took a sip, as Ned watched and waited from the edge of his desk.

"I am not from this time," Jacob said. He placed his cup on the saucer with a clank, and looked at Ned.

"Of course you're not."

Jacob looked up at Ned as the music stopped. Ned looked back at him, resting his chin on his hands, as the clock ticked in the background of the now silent office.

But Jacob now knew.

As if thunder crashed and a flash of lighting bolted through his mind, he could remember the image of his grandmother, lying in her coffin. He could hear the faint organ music playing; he could still smell the sweet spiced aroma of the cascading flowers that surrounded her casket.

Ned took a sip from his coffee, and raised his eyes, looking directly at Jacob. Jacob saw him smile. "You've had an epiphany," he said, setting his cup back on the desk. "Most do at some point."

Jacob's mouth dropped open as his face shifted. "I...I don't understand...and how I got here..." He stared Ned in the eyes as he walked behind the desk and sat across from Jacob.

"How did I get here?" Jacob watched Ned, looking directly at him, pleading. Jacob could feel the uncertainty well within him.

Ned folded his hands on the blotter and cracked a thin smile. "That's a fairly common question as well."

"So do you have the answer?"

Ned leaned back. "I don't have all the answers, Ned. Do you think you came here just to ask me questions that man has been asking for centuries?"

"I'm afraid I don't follow."

"Permit me to explain," he said. The music stopped playing as the needle found static. Ned slowly rose from his tall, smoked leather chair, and closed the phonograph. Only the sound of the ticking clock remained.

"Look around you, Jacob."

Jacob looked all around the room, noticing the fine stained wood appointments; the perfectly tended large plants; the bookcases lined with volumes of books; the artwork hanging on the wall and plush area rug lying on top of a marble floor.

"This place is about…life," Ned said, as he moved to the front of the desk, leaning on the front, crossing his arms and looking down at Jacob.

Ned continued. "But as you already know, all life, one day, must come to an end."

Jacob nodded. "Yes. I learned that very early on."

"Correct," Ned said, as a piano started playing in a distant room.

Ned raised his eyes towards the doors to the foyer, and smiled. "Ah, I hear Rosa playing again. She has been playing for as long as I can remember."

"So, you see," Ned said. "We all wind up here. It's not so much about death. And the uncertainty that surrounds it. But it's really about life. And there are the little intricacies that connect us all – music, art, spirituality. Among others. But here, this is where we all wind up. Our final stop on the endless journey that defines our existence."

Jacob stood and smoothed his jacket as Ned opened the door to the foyer. "I see," Jacob said.

Ned walked into the foyer just as the door chimed. The frosted glass concealed a tall, dark figure. Ned paused for a moment, looked at the door, and then up the winding stairs, but the piano music kept playing.

He headed towards the door and opened it slowly.

A tall, dark skinned man stood at the threshold wearing a long, flowing black coat, nearly down to his ankles. Jacob thought the form of dress was peculiar, considering Miami's year round tropical-weather. The man removed his top-hat and held it at his chest and Ned extended his arm. The man stepped across the threshold and nodded both to Ned and Jacob.

He extended his right hand to Jacob. "Good evening," he said. "I am Antoine Nagevesh."

Jacob shook his hand and smiled politely.

Antoine then looked directly at Ned. "I trust you've received my telegram?"

Ned nodded as Antoine removed his coat. Ned took it and hung it in a nearby closet. He looked over at Jacob. "Jacob, why don't you relax upstairs? I have some business matters I need to discuss with Mr. Antoine here."

Jacob had waited for Ned to return to the upstairs living quarters. Jacob made a modest dinner, set the table for two, and even lit several candles. But then, the sun went down, and Ned still hadn't returned. He cleaned up the dinner, blew out the candles, but left Ned's plate on the table, covering it with a shined, gleaming silver dome.

After retiring, at some point in the night, Jacob awoke. He heard a sliding coming from downstairs.

A grating.

He crept downstairs and padded across the marble foyer in the pale reflected moonlight, and down the hallway to the crematorium entrance. The light was burning. And the stairs leading below were lit with the yellow incandescent light.

He took the steps carefully with a light touch of his feet; but the grating continued. When he saw the opening on the side of the stairs, he ducked behind the railing. He held his hand up to his mouth.

Ned was pushing a dirty coffin along the floor.

It certainly had already been buried. Was Ned digging up caskets? And why?

Mud and dirt trailed from behind it, dirtying the concrete in the headlight field of the running hearse.

Jacob kept his hand over his mouth and watched as Ned grunted, sliding the casket across the floor, closing in on the rear hallway which led towards each crematory chamber room. Jacob took one additional step down, and craned his head around the corner as Ned got closer to the threshold of the dark hallway.

Jacob couldn't face him.

He simply watched as Ned pushed the casket deep into the corridor, and as he disappeared into the shroud of darkness, Jacob crept down the stairs, to the cold, dirty cement floor.

The trail of dirt looked red. Like blood. Oozing from the hearse, deeper into the room, down the darkened corridor of death to the cremation chambers...but why?

He continued further, and hid behind the wall at the threshold of the door to the rear hallway. He could just make out Ned's silhouette against the dim light that emanated from the hearse's headlights...and he saw Ned push the casket into the last room.

Now he remembered.

It was the door to cremation chamber number seven.

But why?

Clarissa, Susan, Darryl and David made it to the downstairs receiving area where the ceiling had collapsed the night before. Darryl and David started moving fallen rafters as Clarissa barked at them to stop.

"We won't find him there!"

They stopped and looked at her.

"Don't you see? We have been communicating with him! The light fixture upstairs...the music we have heard...everything! You won't find him in number seven! But he is here! He is *everywhere!*"

"Stop it!" Susan cried. "Just *stop* it!" She covered her face in her hands and sobbed. Darryl reached over and she collapsed in his arms. He glared at Clarissa.

"Look," David said. "He was just here last night. I'd heard him. And then the ceiling collapsed. How can he *not* be back there?!"

Clarissa looked up towards the gaping hole in the ceiling and smiled. She closed her eyes. "Because I can feel his presence here. Very strong. Indeed." She opened her eyes and looked back at the others. "He is dead. Gone! Don't you see?" She reached out and touched Susan's arm. "Don't you feel it too?"

"He is everywhere!" Clarissa beamed. "The dead communicate…through other ways. Not just speaking to them, or through a Ouija board. Don't you see how Jacob has been communicating with us?"

Darryl scowled. "What do you mean?"

"The mirror," she said. "And the candelabra. Even the music! It's like we can feel his presence all around us here!"

Susan's eyes widened as she tore away from Darryl's arms. The stairs creaked as she ran up to the upper level; Darryl and David quickly followed, but as David looked back, Clarissa was gone.

Just her singing, soft, fading into the distance of the dilapidated wreckage, remained. The three of them stood, looking at each other, bewildered. Susan's mouth dropped open when they realized they were standing there alone.

"Where…did she go?" Susan finally asked as David hoisted a rafter upwards and started clearing the area.

David shook his head and Darryl put his arms around Susan. "He can't be dead," David said. "But Clarissa…how did she?"

"I think she's somehow part of this place," Darryl said, as Susan sniffled. She pulled away from Darryl's arms and shook her head. She looked up the stairs, towards the main level.

Her voice lowered. "If he is still here, we will find him."

BLOOD
HEARSE
PERSONA

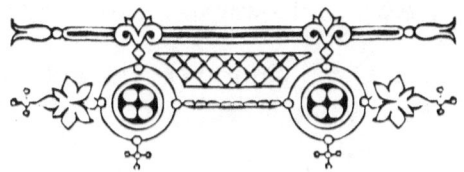

SUSAN BOLTED UP THE CREAKY,
WOODEN STAIRS.

"Susan, come back!"

Darryl yelled ahead and David dropped the
beam as they barreled up after her. They ran
through the coffin elevator room, and headed
down the long, dark hallway to the foyer.

There was Susan, standing in front of the
mirror.

335

She slapped her palms against the wall. "Jacob!" she screamed. "Jacob, I know you're there! We will find a way to get you out!"

Darryl and David ran to her side, and they all watched the mirror.

The reflection lightened, but the physical room in which they stood, behind them, remained the same.

Their mouths were agape as they watched the reflection change.

They saw the marble was well polished; the giant potted palms full, and green.

The foyer within the mirror was bright.

And airy.

So alive.

And then Susan gasped as they saw Jacob appear.

His hair was different; slicked back, parted in the middle. He pulled on a grey blazer as another taller man appeared, holding a red tie. Susan looked over at David, her head titled and her face shifted.

"That's Ned McCracken," he said.

They watched intently as Ned stood behind Jacob, reached around, as Jacob raised his rounded collar, and as Ned reached around and started tying the red fabric in a bow in front of Jacob's neck.

And then Ned turned Jacob's head towards him, and they looked into each other's eyes. Darryl shook his head. "What the – ?"

Jacob and Ned's noses touched, their lips close to touching, as the group watched in silence.

And then Susan gasped as Ned tilted Jacob's head to the side; they could see his jugular vein bulging and pulsating.

Susan looked back at David, her eyes wide, and David covered his mouth with his hand.

She looked back.

Ned caressed Jacob's neck with his finger as an unseen piano started playing Beethoven's *Moonlight Sonata.*

Ned plunged into Jacob's neck as bright red blood flowed down his neck, staining his white shirt like a crimson river.

Susan screamed. "Jacob! Jacob!" She slammed her palms against the wall, as the suckling continued.

And then the image faded, and the mirror returned to the dusty, damaged reflection.

"No!" Susan screamed, running out the front door.

The building shook and quaked, as the piano music hit a crescendo. The rafters cracked and splintered as plaster started to shower on them. Darryl and David rushed towards the front door, and escaped as the ceiling caved in from above, spilling down the front steps; coughing on the dust as the entry was covered in rubble, blocking all further access.

Ned slid the dirty casket inside and slammed the door to crematory number seven. He parked the hearse, slid the large door closed to the receiving area, and snapped the light off.

He headed up the creaky, wooden stairs, back through the hallway, and paused to pull the door closed. He pulled a brass key from his pocket and twisted the lock with an audible click against the silence.

After heading upstairs to the living quarters, he saw Jacob, nestled under the covers, his head deep in the pillows, his breathing quiet and regulated.

The poor boy.

He seemed so inquisitive.

But they all were.

At least when they first came.

But Ned knew that he had to find a worthy successor. Could Jacob be just that?

He'd come to trust Jacob in the time that he'd been there, helping him. The boy was a quick study. And had a talent for the business.

But did he understand what Waxley was really about?

The thunder rumbled in the distance the following day as the showers in the area were getting further away. Sun peeked through the retreating clouds and gleamed a reflection on the drops on the brilliant green tropical foliage in the front gardens of Waxley.

Ned stood in front of the window, pulling apart the long shears, watching the dark clouds retreat. Too much thinking lately.

Too many thoughts.

Save your thoughts for the time in the coffin, mother always said...

And then Ned closed his eyes as his mind fought memories which clamored for attention.

He saw the network of veins; the arm was always there. White. Pasty. And waiting. He remembered standing, as a boy, couldn't have been more than ten.

Back in the days at McCracken, he remembered his father, standing over the preparation table. He always remembered looking up, as he hadn't been so tall back in those days as a child.

There was something about the dead bodies that would pass through McCracken Funeral Home, when Ned's father was still alive and at the helm. Ned would stand up on his tippy toes, his fingers scarcely reaching the edge of the white sheet.

"Neddie...back down. This one hasn't been washed yet."

Little Neddie's eye widened. "You wash the *bodies*?"

His father placed large, black rubber gloves on his hands and pulled them up towards his elbows. He bent over and started massaging the arms, and then legs of the body. He ran his gloved hands up and down, running the length of each limb. After a few moments, he looked over at Neddie. "We wash each and every body that comes through here. Sanitize 'em too. But until we do, there can be bacteria and disease on the dead person's skin. So that's why I wanted you to back down."

The way his father handled the body was so informative, so clinical. Neddie stood against the far wall, leaning on his hands which were clasped behind his back, and watched his father wash the body, as the soap and water ran through the drainage system on the preparation table. His father bent over the body and studied each limb, massaging each arm and leg with the precision of a doctor.

But he also remembered when Stephen had been lying on the preparation table, and he had stood there at the same time, as well, watching father prepare his own son's body.

And things weren't so clinical when Stephen had been lying on the preparation table.

In fact, that was the first time that Neddie had seen his father cry.

"Ned," he said, his voice quivering. "Let me take care of Stephen alone."

But Ned watched through the glass window in the door. He watched as he saw his father remove the white sheet and place a towel over Stephen's midsection. He felt the warmth of tears on his cheeks as his father ran soapy water over his brother's naked body; Ned had watched his father perform this cleaning ritual countless times in the past, he used to scrub the skin; in every finest detail, between the fingers and toes, massaging the skin.

But this time, with Stephen, it wasn't so clinical.

 His father had did the same procedure that he had educated Neddie about previously; he still had used the exact same arm's length black rubber gloves, but when it was Stephen's body lying on the preparation table, things were different.

Loving.

And it was the first time that Ned had seen his father cry.

Jacob dressed and headed down the stairs.

Ned would certainly have some explaining to do.

And now, that Jacob remembered his past – his true past – things were most definitely different. He remembered everything. Maybe it was seeing the dirty coffin sliding across the floor. Or the music the day before.

He wasn't sure what the trigger was.

But he knew he wasn't from that time. Or that place for that matter.

He had previously questioned it; especially when he looked in the mirror. He'd always felt that someone was looking back at him; a different reflection from a different time, but people he had known.

Rosa was in the foyer polishing the marble floor. He looked across to the office; he saw that the doors were open and Ned was already inside, looking out the front window. Jacob approached and knocked softly.

Ned looked over and hastily wiped his cheeks.

"Uh, good morning, Ned."

Ned, nodded and retreated behind the desk. Jacob took the usual wooden side chair and faced his superior.

"Are you alright?"

Ned waved his arm. "It's nothing." His voice quivered. "Please help yourself to some coffee and pastries." He gestured over to the side credenza, as Jacob rose and poured himself a cup of steaming, black coffee in a small china cup, and selected a fresh, hot croissant. He returned to the chair and placed his items on a small side table as Ned took a breath and ran his palms over his face.

"Okay," Ned said. "I have something to show you, Jacob. Will you work a little later this evening? You can stay in my quarters again, if you like. I rather enjoy having you there. But I have some things to show you out at Resurrection."

"The cemetery?"

Ned looked up and nodded. "Yes. Out there."

Jacob hadn't spent much time in cemeteries in his life. He hadn't even remembered burying the coffin after his Gramma's funeral. But then, he was just a child at the time. And the memories that stood out in his mind from that day were what he had thought of... standing on the stepstool next to her casket, reaching out with his tiny finger and touching her cheek.

And drawing his hand back and gasping when she felt so cold to his touch.

"What are you going to show me, Ned?"

Ned breathed in and out through his nose as he put on a pair of work boots. "Dress appropriately," he said. "Get out of your suit. Wear something you can get dirty."

Jacob turned and approached the stairs and looked back towards Ned, who was rummaging through the office. Jacob peered through the partially open doors, and saw Ned behind the desk reaching his arms around the golden frame of the Schubert painting. There was something behind there. Of that Jacob was certain.

But he could not let on that he was watching.

Or was Ned allowing him to watch? He couldn't stand on the steps and ponder the question. For Ned would be expecting him downstairs directly. And Ned didn't like to be waiting. But what was Ned was going to show him out in the cemetery? Jacob went into his room at the end of the living quarters' hallway and opened his dresser drawer. He pulled his suit pants down to his underwear, kicked them off onto the floor, and grabbed a pair of brown work pants and a white short-sleeve from the closet. He opted for the heavy work boots. Within minutes, he was dressed and headed for the stairs.

"Come on, Jacob! We have to get going!"

Ned was calling from downstairs.

Jacob pulled his shoes on and ran down the stairs.

"Jacob!" Ned called. "Come on!" Ned's voice was still in the distance.

One more level down.

Jacob headed down the long hallway, through the coffin elevator room, and down the creaky wooden stairs. The large sliding door was open to the outside, and the hearse was parked in the fading twilight. The headlamps were on, illuminating the receiving area. Jacob paused for a moment at the foot of the stairs. An image of Ned sliding the dirty coffin through the room last night flashed through his mind. So he hadn't been dreaming, after all.

Had he?

Ned stepped outside of the driver's door and waved for him to come to the hearse. "Come on!" he said. "We don't have much time!"

Jacob took a few steps towards the hearse and stopped. "Where are we going?"

Ned let out and exasperated sigh and shook his head. "To the cemetery…*like I told you*. Now get in!"

Jacob did what he was told.

As he sat in the front passenger seat, he looked over at Ned as he got behind the wheel.

He shifted the transmission and the car moved forward.

Ned hummed to himself as they wound around the building, navigating the dirt paths towards the manicured front drive, through the trees, across the long winding road towards Resurrection.

Jacob watched Ned as he turned the giant, black wheel. Jacob now knew. This wasn't his time. Nor was it his place. Everything about the place, about Waxley, seemed…vintage. Like he was in the starring role of an old Hollywood black and white. When he had first arrived, he simply hadn't known. He hadn't realized. Maybe his mind had to catch up, somehow. But it wasn't until recently that he started noticing the little oddities. Like he was out of place. But the feelings weren't there initially. Even when the newspaper had blown across the sidewalk next to the bread lines, he had thought that everything then was normal.

But it wasn't.

And he knew now.

His mind had caught up.

He had been exploring the remains of the mortuary with David. He remembered that specifically. His parents were Clint and Barbara, and he went to school at Nazareth University. He most certainly wasn't from this bygone era.

"We're here!" Ned exclaimed, plunging the large shifting gear towards park. He released the clutch and pulled on the brake.

Jacob looked around and saw the rising crosses and sculpted angels. The sun had almost cleared the horizon; the sky was a faded orange, leading to black, and as Ned got out of the car, he handed Jacob a flame oil lantern.

"Where we are going is over there," he said. His voice sounded louder than usual against the silence of the coming night. He pointed over towards a weathered mausoleum, and as Ned headed through the gravestones, a layer of mist swirled at their feet. Jacob watched as Ned pulled a set of iron keys from his pocket, and they clanked together as he approached the iron gates of the mausoleum.

"Lock's pretty rusted," Ned said, as he jiggled the keys.

Jacob watched as the lock finally clicked, and the gate swung open with a deep creak.

"That man who was here earlier...his name was Antoine. Do you remember him?"

"Yes," Jacob said softly, as Ned pushed the cement door inwards with a deep rumble.

"Well, he has been contracting with me to help him with his population."

Jacob shook his head as he held the lamp for Ned. "Population?"

Ned stopped in front of a crypt. "This one right here will do." He reached outwards and placed another key into the black rusted lock, and turned it. He looked back at Ned and cracked a grin. "Yes. Antoine has...a gift."

"A gift?"

Jacob set the lantern down and leaned in to help Ned with the large, heavy concrete slab.

They grunted and hoisted it on the floor as the casket came into view.

Ned appeared out of breath, and mopped his brow. The flicker of the lantern warmed his skin. "Let's just say that Antoine will never be lying in here."

Jacob shifted his face as confusion took over. It looked out of place. He then looked over at the casket. It wasn't one of the wooden coffins that had been popular in that time. It seemed far more modern. Made of steel, perhaps. More like what he had remembered before he was trapped in the past at Waxley; similar to his Grandmother's coffin.

He took a step back and shook his head. "No…"

Ned chuckled. "Oh no, don't worry. It's just a coffin. And no. Your *Gramma* is not in there."

Jacob looked over at Ned with wide eyes.

Ned smiled. "Don't you see, Jacob? Don't you see what this whole place is about?"

Jacob bit his lip and looked over at the casket.

"She's stainless steel, Jacob. Top of the line. You know, during this time…you know we still bury people in plain wooden coffins? But look in there. A steel beauty. Nothing's getting in there. Now help me lift it into the hearse."

They reached in the crypt and hoisted the casket outside, and placed it on the floor. Ned bent down, picked up the lantern, and held it upwards.

"Open it," he said.

Jacob looked up at him, not knowing what to expect. Ned stood, a smile on his face, watching, as the flicker of the lantern warmed the interior of the mausoleum.

Jacob's hand shook as he undid the latches on the top edge of the casket. He hadn't seen buried remains before. And he could only imagine that the experience would be gruesome.

He closed his eyes as the lid creaked open.

He heard Ned laugh as he peeked. Ned was smiling and shaking his head. "Come around here," he said, gesturing with his free hand. "There's nothing to be afraid of."

Jacob took a breath and held it. He watched Ned look at him warmly from the other side of the open coffin lid. But he'd never stared death in the face so forcefully ever before in his life – whether in his true time or this time. As he rounded the casket, he closed his eyes again, as his heart pounded in his chest.

"Open your eyes," Ned said.

Jacob covered his eyes with his hands, and peeked through the cracks between his fingers. He saw a yellowed glimmer of white satin; the flicker and orange glow of the lantern.

And then he brought his hands down.

"It's empty!"

He looked over at Ned who smiled and nodded.

"Precisely," Ned said, smiling. Now help me load it in to the hearse. We need to take it back to the mortuary."

"Why do you have a modern casket here?"

As they bent down and hoisted up the coffin, Ned made eye contact with Jacob.

He cracked a grin.

They carried it out to the hearse. As Ned slammed the wide back door, he exhaled. And then looked up at Jacob. "It's for a very special occupant," he said, and headed to the front of the hearse.

They left the casket in the receiving room, and Ned parked the hearse. They retreated to the living quarters upstairs, and ate dinner together in silence. Ned read the newspaper as they ate soup and bread, and Jacob couldn't help but watch Ned the entire time, who seemed quite comfortable and at ease.

Jacob slept fitfully that night.

The next day, Ned sat at the desk writing in the files, looking down, and then, put the paperwork down with a flop. "We have another viewing today. They were in with last minute plans early this morning. I chose not to wake you." He glided out of the office, and down towards the viewing room. Rosa was running the vacuum as the workers were hauling a wooden coffin – much more adherent to the time – and setting it on the far wall of the viewing parlor against the windows.

"Um, Jacob."

Rosa cut the power to the vacuum cleaner and looked up.

"Jacob, can I talk to you for a minute?"

He nodded. "Sure."

Ned placed his hand on Jacob's shoulder and took a breath. "Care to join me in the office?"

Jacob nodded and they turned into the hallway that opened to the foyer. Ned went to the wooden double doors next to the large mirror, and drew a key from his pocket. He opened the door and stood back, opening his arm as Jacob took the cue and walked in.

"Have a seat," Ned said.

Jacob sat in a small, wooden chair opposite the large desk. He leaned forward, his arms over his legs.

He held his hat in his lap and watched Ned slowly pull his tall, leather chair out from behind the desk, sit down, lean back, and rest his hand on his chin.

He looked at Jacob.

"Tell me a little about yourself, Jacob."

Jacob stammered and bit his bottom lip.

Ned sensed his nervousness and smiled. "Can I tell you a story?"

Jacob nodded.

"Good then," Ned said. "You know, I know about your reservations about this place. But I can sense that it's a good fit for you, despite your apparent reservations. But the original owner, Everett Waxley, left control of this operation to me after he passed. The Bannister funeral was my first solo event. And as we pass through here, we all remain for different lengths of time."

Jacob's face shifted as he eased himself into the chair. Rosa approached from behind and handed him a glass filled with a brown liquid. Jacob looked at it quizzically.

"It's just rye," Ned said, taking a seat behind the desk in the massive smoked leather chair.

Jacob raised his eyes and looked at Ned.

"Rye whiskey," Ned added.

"Whiskey first thing in the morning?"

Ned leaned forward and nodded. "You're going to need it. It'll calm your nerves."

Jacob downed the whiskey and felt the burn in his throat. He looked across the desk at Ned, who sat there, looking at him, smiling, as the room started to get fuzzy. He nodded and smiled, as Jacob felt himself sliding down in his chair, the room fading to black.

He opened his eyes.

He was lying on the concrete, downstairs, in the bowels of the funeral home. Staring down the darkened hallway leading down to the cremation chambers.

Jacob rose to his feet and felt the cold tiles on the wall with his hands as he eased himself down the dark hallway.

Crematory number seven.

It was down there. At the end of the hall. And in his mind, Ned repeated himself.

What I need to know....is...something about you and the world. Your world. Your life. Do you remember everything? All that you have done?

But there was something different about this world. He had felt that early on. In the beginning, he didn't know. Everything seemed as it always had been, but in the beginning, he didn't know anything different. Had he been placed in another body in another time? He didn't think so.

It is my world. These are my sins. My own personal transgressions.

Jacob looked at each door as he passed. Ned was right. This was his world. The world of deathly existence; of coffins and crematoriums, from which he may never leave, except being carried to the grave in his coffin.

It is my life. What do I do? I never want to stray; I never want to want.

"It's time for you to take over for me. But are you a worthy successor?"

Jacob recalled when they had hoisted Mr. Bannister's coffin into the hearse and Ned leaned against the wide open back door. He pulled off his work gloves and mopped his brow. He was out of breath.

"Well, Jacob? Are you? Ready to take over?"

"What?" Jacob looked at Ned, who was still out of breath. "In this purgatory? Is that what this is?"

Ned caught his breath as he flicked the hearse lights off. "Call it what you will," Ned said. "But we're all sinners. We all do wrong."

But Jacob shook the memories off.

And Ned permeated his mind as he approached the final door.

To crematory number seven.

My mind is flowing freely with these thoughts. But it's the image of the grave.

Those nights when I cannot speak of the images that permeate my mind.

I don't ever want to visit there again.

I don't know. I don't ever want to know what is beyond…in the cemetery.

"Ned, please be quiet," he whispered.

As Jacob approached the door, he could hear a rattling.

And a rumble.

He recognized that rumble. The cremation chamber door was now open.

I don't ever want to visit there again.

There are far too many words.

Far too much blood.

Earlier in the day, Jacob had sipped his whiskey, just as Ned had instructed him.

He looked outside the window, before the whiskey took its effect, and saw a carriage disappear through the trees, closer towards Resurrection.

Another funeral in progress.

And the coffin would be buried. And the body would lie under six feet of ground, and rot for eternity.

Or so the family thought.

He swallowed the burning liquid, and placed his glass back on the side table with a slight clank.

He shook his head.

Of course it wouldn't.

That scenario would never play out in Resurrection Cemetery. Not with Ned at the helm.

And not with Crematory number seven.

I don't want to go there again.

Jacob leaned down and looked at the ground, just outside the door. The roar of the flames shook him, as the orange glisten of the flames highlighted a photo that lay on the rough, dirty cement.

But he recognized that photo.

Ned was still wearing his blue suit; the mortuary was in its prime; the grey shrubs…it was all there. And the memories of when *he* first encountered that photo…in the library at Nazareth University…flooded his mind.

Jacob dropped the photo and looked up at the wall.

His mouth dropped open.

His head snapped to the right as he heard the clip of Ned's shoes on the stone floor. He was approaching the door.

Jacob's heart beat hard in his chest and his breathing quickened as he bent down to pick up the photo. He fumbled with the frame pulling the brass connectors apart. He shoved the photo behind the glass and turned.

Ned was standing in the doorway with a scowl on his face. His hands were on his hips.

"Who gave you permission to come down here?"

Ned slowly showed the photo to Ned. He took a step backwards, and placed his arms outwards. "I..didn't…"

Ned took a step forwards. "Where did you get this?"

Jacob stammered and looked at the floor. "I…it was just lying here on the floor."

Ned scowled and yanked the photo from Jacob's hands. Ned covered his mouth.

Jacob closed his eyes and hung his head. "…look at anything…"

And then Jacob saw the trees. And heard the beating.

Take it you little faggot!

Jacob watched as Ned stood, tears streaming down his cheeks.

Stephen, help me!

Jacob's mouth dropped open as he watched Ned wipe the tears from his cheeks. Ned glared at him. "That's the last time you look in my mind," he said.

Ned lunged forward and grabbed Jacob's collar. "You don't come here unless I tell you to. Do you *understand*?"

Jacob eye's widened and he could smell the formaldehyde on Ned's fingers. He could feel his heart beating fast. Ned had never acted like this before.

His breath smelled sour.

Ned released his collar. "Now go to crematory one. The urn is ready. Go. Now. And then come right back."

Jacob rushed past him and nodded. He looked back, and saw Ned look back down at the photo, looking down at it in his hands.

But it wasn't Ned's outburst that upset Jacob. He glanced at faded green tiles as he rushed past. As he walked down the hallway and towards crematory one, thoughts permeated his mind.

It was now clear.

This wasn't his time.

Nor was it his place.

He could remember now…exploring the ruins of this very building. And he remembered entering the cremation chamber…but little else after that, until he woke up in his apartment.

Decades earlier.

Had it been some sort of a time machine?

A portal to an alternate dimension?

As he hoisted the heavy steel door open for crematory one, it scraped on the cement floor.

He squinted his eyes against the darkness, as just a sliver of light emanated from the dank hallway.

He saw the indiscriminate edge of a casket. It was open, sitting on the floor. The same casket they had unearthed from the cemetery crypt.

And then felt the strength of flat open palms against his back.

He fell forward but caught himself before falling on the hard stone floor and into the casket. He looked up and over his shoulder, as Ned stood in the doorway. He reached over and pulled the string and a yellowish bulb snapped on above them. It was Ned, scowling. He reached down and locked his hands around Jacob's midsection.

"Get inside."

Jacob looked up at the casket and saw Ned standing with pursed lips, his hands on his hips.

"Get *in*!"

And then Jacob's mind reverted.

He saw his mother smiling down at him from the bleachers on the day that he walked for Graduation, his maroon gown blowing in the wind, his honors stole hanging proudly around his neck.

The good, positive thoughts that had permeated his mind.

And the darkness fought through as well.

He held his hands up as Ned blocked the light, and reached down. He lifted him to his feet. Jacob held his breath and looked over at the casket.

Ned shook his head and pushed him over towards the coffin. "They do this every damn *time*!"

Jacob stood and folded him arms.

"Get inside your casket, Jacob! It's the only way! *You have to accept reality.* What it is to *you*."

Ned reached around and tore into Jacob's face, knocking him backwards into the coffin. Ned reached down, panting, and slammed the lid. Jacob reached and felt fresh, hot blood running down the side of his mouth, as he was closed in darkness.

"It's time Jacob." Ned's voice sounded muffled as the coffin lid clicked and locked. "Rest well…"

MISERERE MEI DUES

SUSAN'S SMALL, SILVER, RUSTED SEDAN charged down Ascension Avenue. Her eyes wide, she looked over at Darryl. "We have to go back for him!"

"He's not *there*!" David said from the back seat. "We don't even have any way of clearing the debris to even get to him if he were! Didn't you hear Clarissa?!"

Susan glared at him in the rearview mirror and shook her head. "I'm not giving up so quickly.

And Clarissa just vanished. Makes me even wonder if she was even there in the first place."

Darryl reached over and touched Susan's arm as she pulled the car over. She threw it into park and cut the engine. "Susan," he said. His voice was soft. Calming. "You have to accept the reality of what has happened. You are holding on to him for too long."

She looked over at Darryl, her mouth hanging open, shaking her head. "You mean what has *happened*? Didn't David – I mean *Professor Howell* – go together here with Jacob…unauthorized I might add…to explore this haunted dump?!"

David leaned forward. "Yes. But I only went to protect him!"

Susan snapped her head around. "Look at what that got you!" she hissed.

David raised his open hands. "I am *sorry*. I admit I was caught up looking for all of the supposed secret documents that I don't even think existed! But Jacob wandered off on his own!"

Susan stewed in her seat. A car passed on the street next to them.

"I know the trip wasn't Nazareth authorized," David said. "But I was really only going so he wouldn't have to go alone."

Susan looked up and back at David in the mirror. Darryl turned around in his seat. "We appreciate it, man."

Susan breathed in and out through her nose. She made eye contact with David again. "You could lose your tenure."

"Yes, I know."

"So then you need to help us find him," she said. "We need to come back at first light and climb in there."

David looked down and shook his head. "He's not there, Susan. You're not going to find him that way."

She slammed her hands on the steering wheel. "Why do you keep *saying* that?! He was just there with you!"

David raised his eyes as Susan snapped around, glaring at him. "His presence is all over there. But you guys need to examine your *own* lives and see how much you really remember from

Jacob. And how much you remember because you wanted it to be true. Or if "

Darryl's face shifted and he shook his head. "What are you talking about, man?"

David sighed. "Because you have to realize how Waxley can get into your head. The whole idea of it plays with your mind. Are you really looking for Jacob Benjamin? Or something else?"

"Something *else*?!" Susan shrieked.

But then Darryl knew.

He remembered when he'd first met Jacob. As he sat on the edge of the grass watching the neighborhood children playing dodge ball. And Darryl could see himself, looking down at Jacob, through Jacob's eyes. He saw himself standing in the sun, as Jacob had shielded his eyes. And then Darryl saw himself again through Jacob's eyes, but many years later, on the steps of the Nazareth University Library. There had been the same sunlight penetration...as if a celestial vision. Was Jacob the Angel? Or a vision from the afterlife?

Or was he?

David held up his hands again as Darryl leaned over and hugged Susan.

"Look, guys," he said. "You both have been going on about this special friend Jacob. And he's been with us – interacted with us – so much as we know, for years, right?"

Susan and Darryl both looked back at him and nodded.

"So what I am saying, is what if he were somehow misplaced in *this* time?"

Both Darryl and Susan shook their heads.

"No," Darryl said. "I remember meeting him when we were just kids. We've been best friends for decades. I even helped him bury his dog a few years back."

"Do you know all that really happened?" David asked. "Are you certain it did?"

Darryl scoffed.

"What are you talking about? Of course it happened! I've known Jacob for years! How could you think I'm that crazy?!"

David looked over at Susan, who had grown quiet.

Her eyes fell. "Let's go back tomorrow," she said, staring at David before starting the engine and throwing the car back into gear.

The three of them crashed at Darryl's apartment. They had a few beers together to unwind, but none of them spoke. Susan decided to play *Gone With The Wind* on the TV that night, and, eventually, the guys both passed out in their clothes. The next morning, as the sunlight filtered through the blinds, they each gradually awakened. Susan, who'd fallen asleep on the couch shortly after the credits rolled, stretched her arms over her head. "Time to go," she said. "We have to find him. Or his body. Whatever's left."

One by one, they each brushed their teeth and splashed water on their faces; and as they piled back into Susan's small, silver, rusted sedan, the silence was impenetrable.

Their car made the left turn onto Ascension Avenue as they encountered construction blockades. "What the?" Susan said as she saw the numerous MAC trucks and pay loaders. "What is happening?"

She pulled the car to the side and cut the engine. She flung her door open and rushed out of the car. Both the guys remained in the car and watched as she ran over to the nearest construction worker. They watched her talking with the man, as he pointed in all different directions. She looked back at the car and waved for them to come. They got out of the car and joined her.

"What's going on?" Darryl asked as David shoved his hands into his pockets and looked around at the scene which was very different from just hours before.

"This man here is saying they are demolishing the building!"

Darryl and David looked at the man, who scratched his head underneath his bright yellow hard hat. "Yeah," he said. "This building's been on the schedule for months now. City's been backed up though."

The three of them took a few steps forward and watched as an army of construction workers in flannel shirts and bright orange jackets prepped the area for demolition. They looked forward as a giant, towering yellow crane with a heavy wrecking ball lumbered down Ascension Avenue.

"New owners!" the man called out over the roar of the engine. "Going to rebuild the whole thing! Place was condemned anyway!"

Susan's mouth dropped as she looked over at the remains of Waxley. She shook her head and tore forward.

"No Susan!" Darryl called and ran after her. David joined them.

"Susan, he's not *there* anymore!" Darryl called, reaching her. He grabbed her, hugging her into his arms, as they spilled to the ground. He placed his mouth just close to her ear. "I don't know what to think about what David said…but Jacob isn't there. We would have found him. Just…let it happen. Let it go. Let *him* go."

And Susan looked up, and watched as the wrecking ball smashed into Waxley Mortuary and Funeral Home. The bricks fell apart, as the splinter of wood and steel shrieked through the morning air.

A single, solitary tear streamed down her cheek, as she watched the building reduced to rubble. And then, as they left a bit later, she looked back at the rubble, the plumes of dust rising through the trees.

And then she wondered.

If Jacob had really been there throughout the years. If everything had really happened the way she thought it had.

And then she looked over at Darryl.

Her friend and confidant as long as she could remember. He put his arm around her, and placed her head on his shoulder. And as they approached the car, she raised her head and looked back at the ruins one last time.

Goodbye, Jacob.

AVE MARIA

THERE WAS MUSIC PLAYING.

He could hear it in the background. It sounded like a chorus. Perhaps of angels. Or a deepening of the note like demons. But music, still, nonetheless.

And the darkness that wrapped around him, wasn't so dark. But it wasn't so light, either. It seemed tarnished. But able to be cleansed.

He had thought he was back in Ned's office; that he was sitting across from the expansive desk in the small wooden chair. But he didn't quite know from where it was coming. He opened his eyes, but could see nothing save discernable light; there were patches of darkness, but they were far muted. Almost grey. And wisps of color that flashed past.

And then, as he looked forward, his vision started to adjust.

There was a dark silhouette approaching him. It slowly approached, and Jacob felt that this was the end. This had answered all of his questions that he'd had throughout his life. Had this been the end? Was Waxley some sort of a purgatory?

The figure stopped just short of where he was, though still out of focus.

"Welcome, Jacob."

It was the voice of a male, but it sounded familiar. He didn't respond immediately. Rather, he racked his brain. Yes, the voice sounded familiar. He'd certainly heard it somewhere before. But he couldn't place it.

He thought of the memories he held. Those of when he was a little boy; the time that he only remembered in what would have been the future compared to his most recent memories; and the memories he held from recent days, in the distant past from his childhood.

But the memories that became most prominent in his mind were not those that had formulated in his mind that took place in the future, but rather of two time periods: the period when he remembered his Gramma, and the other period when he was with Ned, the mortician at Waxley.

The other memories were becoming unclear, out of focus, and less discernable. His time at Waxley, however, was penetrating his mind; behaving as if it were the reality that he had always been in.

He pictured Rosa, the artist that she had told him she was, quite clearly in his mind. He remembered his first night at Waxley, the same evening after which Ned had hired him, when Rosa placed her large handbag on her shoulder, and reached out for the large brass handles of the front doors in the marble laden foyer. She looked up and over at Jacob.

"You know, Jacob," she said.

Jacob looked over at her.

"You know…we're all artists," she said.

She shifted her bag to the other shoulder, and stood with her free hand on the door handle.

"Each and every one of us. We all paint. Sculpt. Or write or sing. We paint the picture of our lives through our actions. Sculpt our legacies through what we stand for. It's how we create our lives. And our legacies, for those who follow us."

Jacob nodded, completely bewildered.

"Building a life is, essentially, creating a work of art," she said.

"Like a composition of classical music. We all leave this world, at some point. But our life…and what we do…becomes our legacy. Our colorful palette. The colors that we choose to paint with – be they dark…or light – comprise the masterpiece."

She smiled, and nodded, opened the door, and looked back once more.

"But we are all masterpieces," she said, and headed out.

And then Jacob thought of Darryl. The friend who he'd known since he was a child; the one friend who he could always count on. Their friendship was like the work of Michelangelo; always sculpting; and Jacob thought of Darryl until the mysterious, yet familiar, male voice spoke again.

"And how do you feel about your legacy?"

He came into focus.

It was the same dark-skinned man who had visited Ned recently.

"Antoine?" Jacob asked.

He smiled and nodded.

"Why am I seeing you here?"

Antoine reached out and touched Jacob's shoulder, bringing him closer. "You need…to understand more about what Ned does. It's much more than a funeral director, or a mortician, or whatever you like to call it. But he helps those whose destiny is death, to embrace it. To accept its purpose in their lives."

"What about me?" Jacob asked.

Antoine nodded and smiled.

"You're a special case," he said. "We watched you when you were at your Grandmother's funeral as a little boy. And ever since then, you have been under our watchful protection."

"Are you angels?"

Antoine smiled and shook his head.

"No, we're not angels. But we each have our assignments. Both in life, and posthumously. Sometimes, our assignment is a single soul."

"What are you saying?"

Antoine took a step back. "I am saying that you need to go back to Waxley. You need to complete your assignment. You have a soul that you must help. But first, I have someone who has been wanting to speak with you…"

AFTER+LIFE

THE PHONE RANG and roused Jacob from a deep sleep. "Hello?" he mumbled. He picked up his sleek, black tablet, touched the screen and checked the time. It was still in the middle of the night.

He shifted under the warmth of the sheets as the caller identified himself from the Coroner's office.

The job continued, now after so many years and decades. He looked over at Ned, his hair now stark white, long, down past his shoulders. So old for this world.

Ned rubbed his eyes and flung the covers from over his legs. "Where is it? Coral Gables?"

He let out a deep breath and sighed. He reached over and nudged Jacob on the back. "It's time for another one. I can sense it."

Jacob nodded. "Yes. It's time."

After Jacob pulled a hoodie on over his t-shirt, he grabbed his keys and flipped the garage light on. The hood of the hearse gleamed against the harsh overhead lighting. He winced and held his arm over his eyes as he trudged over to the driver's door.

A mortician's job never really ends.

There is a time, after the casket is lowered, and the mound of dirt grows, that there may be a short period of rest. But it never will last. For the calls will come. They will continue to come, in the middle of the night, for death never rests.

As the engine roared to life, he backed from the driveway and adjusted the rearview mirror.

He paused for a moment, his eyes staring back at him in the dim interior light. There was a certain feeling that washed through him. A certain numbness; of a life once lived. Of spirits speaking to him from beyond the grave. Speaking of a night filled with death and decay; of a destructive force that continued to eat at him; through his body, his mind and his soul.

But such was a dark life.

There were always bodies to be claimed.

To be placed in the dark bags, zipped and sealed from the activity of life.

And as he arrived at the scene, a small condo on the twenty seventh floor, he stepped into the small bathroom, and saw the body splayed out, a young woman sitting on the toilet, head tilted back, blood splattered on the wall behind her, her eyes gouged out.

There was a detective and deputy standing in the bathroom doorway. He detective immediately looked at Jacob and nodded. He extended his hand.

"Martin Jensen," he said. "I understand your Ned's protégé?"

Jacob smiled and nodded, but said nothing. Detective Jensen returned his attention to the body splayed over the toilet, and leaned in closer towards Ned.

"Look at her eyes," Detective Jensen said.

Ned looked over at her head as he lay the black body bag out in the hallway floor. "Do you think this was self-inflicted?"

Ned leaned in closer.

"No," he said, as the Deputy handed him a steaming cup of coffee. Detective Jensen took another bite of his doughnut.

Ned waved crumbs away as he got up and leaned in closer over her body.

He gasped as a tiny white worm slithered out of her eye, down her cheek and into her open mouth.

"You see that?" Detective Jensen asked, spraying crumbs.

Ned nodded.

"Who's this one?" Detective Jensen asked.

Ned looked over at Jacob and cracked a smile. "Oh, he's a newbie, but he's good. This line of work is clearly meant for him."

Detective Jensen looked at Jacob as he held his coffee in one hand, a half-eaten donut in the other. Ned took a sip of his own coffee.

"We have a lot of homicides in this city," he said. "You think you can handle Miami?"

Jacob raised his eyes and nodded. He reached down towards the body bag as he adjusted the zipper. He looked up at the Detective. "Of course I can handle this."

There was certainly something unsettling about this one. This middle of the night case, the case that had been so different from the countless others that he had answered the phone in the wee hours of the morning for. This one, he knew.

As soon as Jacob looked at the coroner's paperwork, he knew that Darius had been involved. In her death, he doubted. But in her life, he was certain. Jacob could remember paging through the files, talking with Antoine at great length about Darius. About the lovers they were in life, and in death.

Jacob zipped the body bag and Pat helped him hoist her onto the gurney. There was a gurgle. Martin snapped his head down towards the body bag as a slight hiss emanated from deep within.

Jacob raised his eyes at Ned.

"It's common for newly deceased bodies to gurgle and hiss as gases are dispelled," Ned explained.

Jacob grinned. "He's the eternal professor."

Detective Jensen looked up and grimaced.

And then Ned, along with Pat, hoisted up the gurney, its unoiled gears emitting an audible squeak against the otherwise silent apartment. The police had finished their investigation for the time being; evidence had been gathered and bagged and tagged and submitted. Detective Jensen had already left as they wheeled the body out the front door into the brilliance of the Miami sunlight.

The light that faded to the darkness. And faded to black. The time in the coffin. The forever time.

The forever black.

I will resurrect you on the last day…

He promised.

For when the body bag was hoisted into the hearse, and they slammed the door, Jacob watched as Ned looked up at the tall building. Up on the twenty seventh floor. That tiny little bathroom. Those mysterious worms. They slammed the front hearse doors and Jacob looked over towards the passenger seat. Ned looked up at the tall condo skyscraper, a dark, rectangular silhouette rising up into the fading sunlight. Jacob watched as Ned revealed his thoughts. For Ned knew it was time.

Ned remembered when Darius approached him, telling him of his psychological sessions, and how he seemed to always be at odds with Ms. Claire.

But the movement he saw.

That…he couldn't get out of his mind.

There was something quite different about this case. This case. And he couldn't get the thoughts of out of his head.

Could she be? Could she be one of us? Could she have been one of us…all along?

Jacob nudged Ned's shoulder. He looked over.

"You bringing her back to Waxley?"

Ned leaned back in the seat, rolled his window down, and lit a cigarette. He took a drag and blew a cloud of smoke out of the window. "Of course," he said. He looked over at Jacob and met eyes. "There's more to this, you will see. More than just ushering them into the afterlife. It's just like Antoine said. They're all on a quest for immortality. We give them one last shot at Waxley. What they choose to do with that opportunity…is up to them."

"What makes you think that she wants that?"

Ned shrugged his shoulders. "One never knows for sure. But they make their choice once they receive their second chance. The renewed life. Whether or not they choose to stay, that's up to them. That's out of my hands."

"And if she doesn't want it?"

"There's always an option where she could be exterminated. But Antoine has never had to take that path. Everyone he has managed to resurrect has chosen their new path."

And then Jacob pulled the hearse out into traffic, and set the destination for Waxley. After a few minutes of driving, as Ned was puffing on his cigarette, he lowered his window and flung his arm over the side. He looked over at Jacob. As they pulled to a stop sign not far from the mortuary, Ned looked over at him with tired eyes.

"I trust you, Jacob. It's time for you to assume control of the operation."

And then Ned collapsed in the seat.

His eyes closed, his head hit the edge of the open window, lying gently, leaning outwards. The lit cigarette fell to the floor as Jacob gasped and pulled the hearse to the side of the road.

"Ned!" Jacob screamed. He reached out and shook his shoulder.

Jacob rushed to the passenger side, opened the door and eased him to a lying position on the ground. "Ned!" He started CPR compressions, but it was no use.

For Jacob knew what was happening.

It was time.

Jacob leaned down, and embraced Ned. He placed his ear close to Ned's mouth. And there was no breathing.

Jacob leaned back, and felt a tear stream down his face. So many years with Ned. So many viewings. And burials. And dinners together. But Jacob had remembered what Antoine had told him. And what Ned had been grooming him for.

Someone had to carry on the work.

And as Jacob reached down, carrying Ned by his shoulders back to the waiting hearse parked at the side of the lonely street he thought nothing of the onlookers who watched on the busy Miami downtown streets as he dragged Ned out through the marble lobby of the busy condo hi-rise in Brickell, Ned's long, white hair mussed and covering his face and closed eyes. For then Jacob knew.

For in actuality, Ned hadn't even made it to the hearse.

He'd collapsed in the small apartment, right when the zipper ticked closed on the body bag.

I bid you farewell, dear Jacob...

The conversation in the hearse was a gift. One final chat. But Ned was already gone. For when they were in the apartment, Ned had crossed over. Here one minute, gone the next. And Jacob stopped when he realized he was performing CPR on a corpse.

Jacob hadn't even realized – his mind had not accepted Ned's death – when he placed Ned's body in the passenger seat. And started driving. And then had a conversation with him. "You don't always know what's real and what's not," Ned said. "But what's important, is that you maintain your course. Your direction. What was meant for you."

And as he dragged Ned's body towards the back of the hearse, and hoisted the body up into the back, he slammed the door.

Goodbye, old Ned.

And took one final drive to Waxley.

Rosa was waiting at the top of the steps, her hands clasped against her waist, a pained look on her face. Jacob pulled the hearse in front of the steps, and Rosa ran down. She plastered herself against the rear window, looking in at Ned.

Jacob cut the engine and rushed around and placed his arm around her.

"He looks so peaceful," she said, sniffling. "Like I've never seen him before."

Jacob rubbed her shoulder and she looked up at him. "Come with me, I'm taking him down below."

Her eyes widened and Jacob nodded.

They got inside as Jacob turned the key and the hearse roared to life. They took the last trek around Waxley, down towards the lower level and receiving area, down towards the cremation chambers.

Rosa touched his arm. "Number seven?"

He looked over at her and nodded.

Later that day, Jacob stood in the office, leaning over the desk, his weight on his hands.

"I'm going to handle things differently around here," he said. He looked up. "Rosa!"

She appeared moments later as the double doors slowly clicked open. She stood and nodded.

"You no longer have to wear that uniform," he said. "You can wear what you want."

Her mouth dropped open. "Sir?"

"And stop calling me sir. You can call me Jacob."

Jacob moved around the desk until he was standing just in front of her. He placed her hands on his shoulders. "How much time do you still have here with me?"

She lowered her head. "I'm not sure."

He reached out and lifted her chin. She looked up at him.

"I know you are an artist," he said.

Her eyes widened. "Yes...I am."

"So then that's how I want to express yourself around here."

"I...is that...?"

"It's however you feel comfortable," Jacob said. "But I remember our chats. And how you like to sculpt. And paint. You should bring that here. Because that's a part of you." The stained glass doors in the viewing rooms flashed through his mind. "Like the colors on the stained glass in the viewing rooms," he said. "This place needs more color. More of your artwork."

She smiled and nodded. "Thank you sir – I mean Jacob. You are going to be the best one I have worked with, I can tell!"

"The best one?"

She held the door, looking back at him, her smile beaming. "Yes, the mortician. I've worked with so many. You come and go. But I become close with each one in different ways. With you, I can tell it will be different. Maybe that's what we needed around here. Someone like you."

Jacob stood and watched Rosa retreat into the foyer, and close the door. He stood over the desk, his hands shoved into his pockets, and smiled. There was something about this place that intrigued him, even after losing Ned.

He knew Ned had passed him the torch.

He went over to the window and looked out at the brilliant green and colorful gardens. "I am the Mortician," he said to himself. It felt odd to hear it against the silent office.

I am The Mortician…

Jacob remained at the windows and held the big, heavy drapes open. The sun was shining, brilliantly it seemed, brighter that he had remembered it since coming to Waxley. He still remembered the life he had led. There was nothing taking him away from it. He could see himself outside the windows, in the days when

Waxley was crumbling, his young college self…seeking his thesis topic.

Those days seemed so far away; so much simpler. But with a different purpose. And he knew the purpose now was something he was born to do.

He thought of Gramma.

And the day when he stood on the stepstool next to her coffin.

There was a knock on the door.

"Come in," he said, still looking outside.

The steps were slow, methodic, heavy…but determined. Jacob knew. He had remembered those heavy footsteps, but they had seemed so far away for so many years.

And now, he was hearing them again.

He reached up, and covered his mouth, as a single, solitary tear streamed down his cheek.

He turned around.

And there she was.

Just as he had remembered her.

"You touched my cheek," she said as she approached him. Her smile was warm. She was radiant; glowing. She stood behind him, and placed her hand on his shoulder. "You don't know how much I wanted to reach up and touch you back, but I couldn't in that world."

Jacob turned and wrapped his arms around her. He placed his head on her shoulder as he felt the warmth of tears flow. "Oh, *Gramma...*"

She patted his back. "I've been here, the whole time."

Jacob's mind returned to the day he had remembered as a little boy; the day when the streets were frozen and his parents had red-rimmed eyes.

There was a certain feel to the air after Gramma's funeral.

Little Jacob held his Father's hand; they walked to their car, which sat across the frozen parking lot. Jacob didn't remember much after that. Very little snippets. He remembered his father tapping the roof of the car, to show him the small, orange FUNERAL flag that was on top of their car, just like the limousines, and just like the others who came to Gramma's funeral.

No more choo-choo, little Jacob.

But that didn't matter.

As for the choo-choo, that wouldn't happen anymore.

With anyone.

Embrace the life you are given and craft your legacy...

For just after the funeral, at the wake, Jacob's mother attempted to do the same thing that her mother in law had; but it failed.

He grasped his throat, his eyes wide and panicked.

Father turned him over on his knees, slapping him on the back, as others gathered around. Looks of worry and panic spread throughout the gathering.

The paramedics were called, mother was screaming through tears as the wake was interrupted.

But there was a certain light; it emanated against the solitude of the darkness.

It was as if there was a hum of the angels; a warmth, a loving embrace.

And he saw everything.

He saw his family and his friends; digging his dog's grave and exploring Waxley. And then he knew, his work was only just beginning.

And he closed his eyes.

And that was the precise moment when the story really began.

The Astral Files will continue

Did you enjoy *The Mortician?*

Please take the time to submit a review on Amazon, Barnes and Noble, or one of the many worldwide booksellers. Independent Authors like myself count on honest reviews for feedback so we can write more and better stories for you, the reader, in the future.

Did you just discover the writing of A.L. Mengel with *The Mortician?*

He is also the Author of *The Tales of Tartarus* and *The Vega Chronicles*, all of which are available on Amazon, Goodreads, Books-A-Million, Barnes and Noble and various booksellers worldwide.

Follow A.L. Mengel on Facebook, Twitter, YouTube, Goodreads and Instagram. He welcomes interactions with readers, which are called "Beloved Friends" in *The Writing Studio,* a nickname for his Facebook page.

Visit www.almengel.com for news and updates.

The Mortician is Copyright © 2017 Mengel, A.L.

Published by Parchman's Press

OTHER TITLES FROM PARCHMAN'S PRESS

Excellence In Fiction

FIND US ON FACEBOOK

An abandoned immortal raises his maker from a centuries old grave to hellish consequences and uncertainty about his maker...but also himself: is he good...or evil?

ASHES

ANTOINE GATHERED HIS EQUIPMENT - a shovel, brown tarp, pickaxe (in order to pry open the casket) and a flame oil lantern; carefully and quietly he entered the graveyard through a layer of swirling, early morning mist - the type of white cloudy mist that would leave a layer of dewdrops on the earth like a cool, wet blanket. The plot Antoine headed toward, located in the center of the

412

graveyard, housed Darius' casket, encased for two centuries now in layers of earth - sealed by six nails, and placed in a thick cement liner with a crest of a lion on the marble-topped cover.

It was Antoine who put Darius here two centuries ago, and Darius has been in this graveyard ever since. In this cemetery and dead, yes – Darius was dead. But Darius had been dead before Antoine had ever put him there. And when the coffin was nailed shut, when the darkness enveloped satin interior, there was more of changing a state of existence.

It was Darius who had heard the nails being pounded into the edges of the casket; he had felt the shaking as the coffin was picked up – most likely with ropes tied below the bottom, but he couldn't know for sure – and lowered into the deep, dark grave. He had felt the sides of the coffin scraping the cold, hard earthen walls. The dirt fell onto the lid of the casket – each shovel of earth inundating the coffin further with a deep clump.

Blackness.

The sounds from above now seemed more distant. The coffin had been buried. Darius knew that. He even felt the weight of the dirt above him, as if the entire casket would fall on top of him in a cascade of splintering wood and falling sand. But it held. The coffin was holding fast against the pressures of the earth, and would prove to be his holding place for…how long?

The stagnancy of the air inside the small confines grew more insistent, as the heat overtook the darkness and caused him to cough and choke on the thickness of the air that was so quickly fading. But Darius knew. He knew that no matter how fast the air would dissipate, no matter how faint the sounds of the earth above would be – no matter how *dead* he would be – he would be just that.

Dead.

But death is just a state of existence. And Darius knew - all too well - that his death had been many, many years ago – and not so recently in his foyer.

His death had been much earlier when he was a very young man passing into his newfound immortality. Not at the hands of Antoine.

As time passed, he became more aware of his surroundings, although all he saw was total darkness. He could feel the softness and smoothness of the satin liner, the pillow at the head of the casket - which grew hard and cold over time and dusty with mold.

Above where he lay, Darius on occasion could hear the faint, muffled voices above the cold ground expressing words of condolence, the grating of a casket being lowered into a freshly dug grave, or the pitter patter of children's feet; ceremonial instruments would play from time to time, signifying the passing of a loved one. All this, he experienced, lying in the cold darkness of the casket, as time passed by above.

Time passed with an eternal slowness until Antoine returned.

At one point, Darius knew the time had come. He continued to lie in the casket as he felt and heard snippets of the outside world over time, but there was one quiet day when he heard those familiar footsteps; the methodic, determined stomps coming closer and closer to his unmarked resting place. The footsteps stopped, just above. Darius could sense it. He knew who it was. No one knew of his grave except one soul. Only one.

Antoine.

An immortal who lost his gift races against time to avoid a final and permanent death.

THE QUEST FOR IMMORTALITY

DOUGLAS KAHN AWOKE with a start.

He shot up in bed, covered in sweat, and rubbed his eyes, burying his face into his hands. He had been dreaming of the bodies again.

He swung his legs over the side of the bed, and looked at the clock. It was still hours before dawn, and he knew that shortly he would have to put on the black suit that was hanging in the hotel room closet. He closed his eyes and exhaled, running his hands through what was left of his silvery, stringy hair.

He got up, slowly, and walked over to check the air conditioner. He felt the cool air blowing from the vents, but it stopped there. The humidity in the small, boxy hotel room was just stifling.

He poured himself a small glass of bourbon from the mini-bar, and picked up the phone. But he didn't call the front desk.

"Jim?" He took a sip and set the glass down on the bedside table. "Sorry to call you, Jim, but I had the dream again."

"What do you mean?"

"I mean it was just liked it had happened when I was in Miami...the streets...everything. I had passed out in the limo, and when I woke up, the bodies were just everywhere. I couldn't even get out of the car."

"And where was I?"

Douglas stopped for a moment, as his eyes scanned the room. He saw shadows against the wall, set by the warm, pale glow of the exterior hotel lights. "You...I think you were dead."

Jim laughed. "Doug, you have been having this dream for a while now. Doesn't mean a thing."

Doug closed his eyes and shook his head. "Look, Jim. Let's just cancel this trip. I have no idea what it means, but I have known Sheldon for a long time."

"Sure you have."

Doug reached for a cigarette, placed it in his mouth, and flicked the lighter. It wouldn't light after several attempts. He tossed the unlit cigarette back on the table. "Look, Jim, I don't want to go. I have talked with Sheldon so many times before he died, and I know about all the weird shit that he was into. I mean, The Astral was one of the strangest things he ever did. And that Antoine guy...I don't even know what to say about him. But this dream, Jim...I just don't know how to explain it."

"Like it was a prophecy?"

"Exactly."

"So we don't go then. When you go down to the lobby at 8am, like you always do, I will make sure not to be there."

Doug placed his hand over his chin. "I don't know if that's the solution. I still have a lot I have to do down here. The reading of the will, everything."

"So then I should be there? Waiting for you outside the lobby as usual? You need to decide whether you're going or not, Doug."

There was a moment of silence on the line as Doug attempted to light his cigarette again, now with a book of matches he had fished out of the drawer next to the Holy Bible. "Doug? Are you there?"

Doug waved the match and treasured the hot smoke as it flew to his lungs. A small trail of smoke rose to into the air. He exhaled deeply, closed his eyes, and sighed. "Yes, that will be fine. That will be just dandy. Be there at 8. I have an appointment at 9. You know how the Dolphin gets."

Jim chuckled on the other end of the phone. "I sure do, Doug, I sure do. See you then."

They hung up from the call. Doug looked down at the cigarette as it burned in the ashtray; the cherry red tip shone through a plume of ash as the sweet smoke continued rising towards the ceiling. Doug had not touched the cigarette since his initial drag. He didn't even want it anymore. He looked at the clock. It was almost 4am. Jim would be here in four hours.

He extinguished the burning cigarette and slid back under the covers. He desperately wanted to fall asleep, he wanted rest without dreams; he wanted it to be how it was when he and Sheldon were in college, back in the days in Boston, back when life was simpler, before Sheldon followed the path beyond theology and into the darkness.

But Douglas knew better.

The immortal community bands together against a hooded figure who is determined to wipe them out of existence.

THE BLOOD DECANTER

THERE WAS A CERTAIN TIME, and in a certain place, that they knew when they were being hunted.

The rumors had, in fact, been true. They had been

circulating for decades, but were never taken seriously.

Until the one precise moment when the revelation came.

But the knowledge of their potential demise did not come so easily; for it was months, if not years, of research, relationship building, and foraging trust missions where the truth had been revealed: the immortals were, undoubtedly, being extinguished.

And a small, bulbous crystal decanter was the culprit.

The decanter was thought, for a great while, to be the key to eternal salvation. There were many who had talked about it, and about the mysterious one who carried the decanter, who would visit the immortals in time of need; and the one who carried the decanter visited those immortals who were stripped of their gift, who lay dying and aging, heading towards a quick and final death. The decanter was viewed as the ultimate salvation; a catalyst to continue the gift, to add to the dark destiny for which they had been chosen.

But that was a fallacy.

Those who drank from the decanter did *not* find the solace that they desired; they did not receive the expected gift. They did not regain their immortality or strengthen or increase their intelligence. There was an utter agony which propelled itself on them. An infection filled with anxiety, torment, and a slow and painful death.

There were no gifts. There was no salvation from the decanter.

One of the most recent who drank the swirling, hot, red potion lay motionless on the sidewalk outside the Ponce de Leon after sunset, when the night was still in its infancy; lying still and motionless, eyes closed, and the blood still dripped from his mouth.

But he was still as if dead, eyes shut tight, and the young man, and his unkempt hair and sullied clothes, did nothing to represent the individual he had been in life – for he had once been quite fashionable. The torn, dirty pants, should they have been removed, sewn and cleaned, would be seen as of the latest fashion, and could be seen hanging in one of the upscale boutique shop windows that were a mere few steps from where the man lay.

Above where the man lay stood the one who wielded the decanter, who appeared to be a man – a 'Hooded Man' in a long, flowing, dark cloak – who would visit, shortly before death (as it was argued). Here, above the motionless, bloodied man, the 'Hooded Man' stood, watching and waiting, as the white mist that swirled around him abated. As the cloud

425

retreated, so did the man. He walked without motion, with no bending of the knee; as if he were floating or levitating along the ground, and once his duty had been complete, he left.

He was the one who had crossed the world for decades, undetected until recently, the one who had been, for so long, a mythical figure who was thought to bring life eternal, and now was found to bring death.

Can the immortals be redeemed? The story of a warrior, a protector, and confidant: a battle of Good versus evil.

WAR ANGEL

THERE ONCE WAS A STORY of a '*War Angel*'.

When the story had first been told, there were the many questions that followed. There were those who did not understand who the *War Angel* could be. While many wondered, there was an equally significant amount of people who were entirely unaware. But the questions remained, particularly in those societies who had a spiritual and cosmic connection. They asked the questions, over and over. Who is the angel?

Who is this mysterious, mythical angel of battles?

Was the angel male?

Female?

Did the *War Angel* walk among us? Protect us?

Stories had started to circulate among the populace. There were some people that claimed to have seen angelic figures and spirits, particularly at night. Pale, white ghostly apparitions in trees, watching them.

As if waiting for something.

Or someone.

But no one could be for certain if the phenomenon were a product of the *War Angel*. No one could tell if he (or she) were simply observing.

Or protecting.

And then there was the story of the immortals.

And their similar musings of the *War Angel*, and those same supernatural phenomena. The immortals, who had been peacefully coexisting with the humans for centuries, had come to a precipice in their existence: for they were dying and close to extinction. And so the same rumors of the *War Angel* started to circulate through their communities.

The same dinner table talk that the humans discussed penetrated their existence.

Initially, they were just stories.

Stories of angels.

And of demons, and of ghosts.

Throughout time, the stories had fueled the dinner table chatter among the immortals and humans alike. The immortals were on the brink of extinction after dealing with years of torment at the hands of the 'hooded man'. Some of the immortals had wondered who the *War Angel* could be. Perhaps a warrior to protect them? To triumph in their pursuit of goodness?

But the immortals had not been the harbingers of good. And there was no rest for the wicked. For centuries, the immortals were connected with sin.

And evil.

Debauchery and poison.

The humans who befriended them often found untimely deaths. And when they did not, those humans typically had great misfortunes befall upon them.

People started to talk about the immortals.

That they were sinful.

And that those humans who befriended them were courting evil; that those people who became embroiled in the wickedness deserved their fate.

Over time and recent decades, as the immortal society neared total collapse, there had been the advent of a mythical figure called *The Hooded Man*, a malevolent destroyer of the immortal foundation.

While no human being had ever been reported to have seen the robed figure, the rumors, which had initially circulated through the immortal communities, filtered over towards the human population, and not long after, were discussed in government meetings, on news stations, and media.

Immortals Targeted for Annihilation the headlines screamed. Artists painted renditions of *The Hooded Man* from long discussions with their immortal friends.

In Miami, which had long been thought to be the central battleground of *The Hooded Man's* wrath, immortal Antoine Nagevesh, who headed that "sector" of their society, had led a local effort, in joint conjuncture with the human population, to hunt down the hooded figure and destroy him before the immortals were wiped off the face of the Earth.

His drive made it across the Atlantic to France and Rome, where a large concentration of immortals lived, but it became futile. For *The Hooded Man* cast a seductive spell, and Antoine saw that the immortals were destined to wind up where they did: near extinction.

And so came the mystery of the *War Angel* in the society of the immortals. At the council of *The Inspiriti* in Rome, an enlightened society thought to be governed by a council of immortals, there were many discussions. Several members of the high council met over the course of decades to confer the possibility of a warrior, of an angel, and whether the angel posed a threat to the immortals or if it could be an ally.

And others, immortals and humans alike, argued about the mystery.

The *War Angel*.

Who could it be?

The apparitions continued.

Many during times of great distress.

Why the apparitions now? At this time? At this moment when the immortals were on the cusp of extinction? Certainly this being could not be sent to combat the immortals.

Could it have?

And so the questions circulated.

Did he or she travel along the sidewalks, and take a similar journey as the immortals and the people…or did he or she ride a horse?

Or was the story of the *War Angel* possibly in a modern time?

And did he or she sit in automobiles, ride on trains and ships and airplanes, and travel next to us…watching us…without our awareness of their presence?

Many questions permeated minds throughout the world.

And then, after the period of speculation, would follow the mystery of the angel's existence.

There were rarely answers, but the questions would always remain, regardless of the time period or amount of technology in the search: Would the angels only be seen in fleeting moments in times of distress?

Or could they be engaged with human beings in mundane, everyday situations, without our knowledge? Could the next interaction one were to have with another person be a conversation with an angel?

Or even a war angel?

The phenomenon remained a mystery.

There were those who did not understand who the *War Angel* was – nor did they choose to believe in something that they could not see nor prove.

And then, due to the lack of conviction, the world continued to evolve; man discovered science, and evolution. Industry, and technology.

The idea of a spiritual journey – and spirits who were sent from the celestial dimensions to protect – seemed increasingly foreign.

So the questions remained.

Was the war angel really there? Or was it an idea of stories and prayers?

For he or she who the angel was called to protect – would they *see* the angel? Would they even *know* the angel was there fighting a battle in their name?

Initially, there was no acknowledgement.

And complacency reigned, within the immortal populace but the human beings as well. Stories of the War Angel faded as time wore on.

Over the years, some did not believe the war angel actually existed. Man adopted the scientific mindset, and the world evolved. The Industrial Revolution proved to man – at least to a degree – that man was the 'Supreme Being'.

That man ruled the Earth.

God was not the ruler.

God was not the spiritual entity He once was; for man became increasingly self-absorbed.

The seven sins were prevalent. And because of that, man suffered the consequences.

According to Biblical history, Adam and Eve, after committing the first sin, were cast out of Eden, and ever since that time, a time which man had been birthed in the created World, there had been the stain of sin on man, like a fingerprint on a clean surface.

But the stain could be wiped clean.

It could be absolved, there *was* a method of cleansing.

Of redemption.

Man was given "free will" by God. And man, as a general entity, chose to focus on themselves. But that did not mean that man denied God, but, perhaps, rather, did not acknowledge Him. But He was always there, and He still gave man the tools needed for their survival – both physical and spiritual.

And then came a war angel.

A battle assigned angel.

One given to each and every living soul; in many cases (most, if not all cases) the presence of the war angel was completely undetected.

Their presence was ignored, and all spiritual connection was extinguished – and those who were to be protected continued their lives without any awareness of the war angel. But, and it was argued over generations, the war angel was still there, fulfilling their duties.

The story of the *War Angel* was told through generations – it was told again, and again, and again; over the centuries, no matter how many times the story had become diluted, it always reached the same conclusion.

And left the same questions.

Did the war angel actually exist?

Stranded colonists in a post-apocalyptic world seek a habitable zone after the Earth's rotation has stopped.

THE WANDERING STAR

MANY OF THOSE who remained living on the planet Earth could still remember the days when the oceans shifted towards the poles, and when the sea levels rose, higher; seemingly before their eyes; but certainly within a generation.

For the citizens of the United States of America, their memory of the water shifting was real and recent, and even years and decades later, many would recall the Great Shift. It became dinner table talk; bedtime stories. Those who were too young to remember the period of the Great Shift were told of the days when the wave came.

And in those days, it was when the mass exodus from the Northern states was plastered over every news channel; every blog; throughout the internet and on every street corner. In the years during which the shift took place, and as the rotation of the planet slowed, the coastal population was forced to relocate to inland cities. Those in the Northern Hemisphere (and equally so in the Southern Hemisphere) would relocate a short distance from their previous coastal residence, and then, several years later, would be forced to move once again, as the sea crept closer…and closer…to the population. As the planet slowed even further, and it became inevitable for those located nearest to the poles that their cities were slowly being inundated and swallowed by the Earth's waters, it came to a point that entire countries had to be abandoned as great cities were reclaimed by mother nature.

The people of the planet recalled watching in horror as the waters retreated from the tropical zones and spilled towards the north. It wasn't until the northern cities were completely swallowed, and each metropolis would fall into memory and would lie beneath vast depths of seawater, that the inhabitants of the remaining dry areas towards the equator felt the twinge of uncertainty.

Until then, when the cities were lost, it had simply been disbelief. Some cites, like Atlanta or Rome, with a more southerly location, were not spared entirely from the assault of the waters, but the skyscrapers, and some crests on taller buildings rose from the sea. Those cities were partially inundated and still abandoned. Others, closer to the poles, were completely submerged – under a mile of water in some cases, and sentenced to decompose in a watery grave.

London, New York, Toronto, and Moscow – all were lost. Santiago, Sydney, Cape Town…all underwater.

Forever.

Space explorers band together on a mission to excavate through Jupiter's moon Europa's layer of ice to search for life.

THE EUROPA EFFECT

THE STUDY OF THE COSMOLOGY of the Universe had been overlooked in the latter days of the planet. It was when the days on the Earth had turned away from the exploration of the distant and the interstellar; and on the planet, the appreciation of music, and of art, and of philosophy, had waned.

It was during those years when there had been a transformation of such. A transformation of the human minds; but also, physically, of the planet; not only in the geology and the geography of the world, but also a change in the thought process of the people who populated the planet. Their beliefs, motives, and culture.

The long period of the shift had continued for generations…the subtle changes were initially ignored. But over the years, and as the generations progressed, the planet gradually re-terraformed itself. The period of the shift, which had been considered "long" based on the percentage of a typical human life, was insignificant on a cosmic scale.

And that period had become a quest for survival.

After the period of what became known across the planet as the *Great Shift*, those who remained had been labeled "the survivors" and those who perished were remembered. And the world changed drastically in the generations that followed.

During those years, man rarely looked up towards the Heavens. Those times on Earth had become a period of survival, and the thoughts of the cosmos were forgotten.

Until the day when a man had arrived unexpectedly to a colony known simply as "Sector B". He had been disheveled and dirty, physically near death as he had staggered towards the colony's outer doors. Those who had witnessed his approach recalled watching his silhouette against searing sunlight, which had cast radiation on the planet in those days. The man, the scout, had collapsed on arrival, seemingly near death. The colonists risked exposure and rushed to his side, saw that he was still living, and had him taken to medical. Over the following weeks he was nursed back to health, and was known through the colony population as 'the scout'.

Rumors traveled through the colony about what the scout's purpose was.

And when the scout was well enough to speak with them, the people of the planet were urged to look up towards the sky once again: for there was a message.

There was a beacon of hope; of light.

There were those who claimed they had seen a star; and also rumors of those who were thought to have spoken to a mystical star with a message.

And the message was survival.

They believed that the human race could live on, if they looked upwards and outwards. Their destiny was not to remain living underground with dwindling rations, heading toward extinction.

It was to journey outwards.

To reach beyond.

To trust, and to take a leap of faith.

But the aura of the planet had indeed changed. Culture had vanished; no longer were there orchestral performances in city centers; many artistic masterpieces were lost forever under the sea in cities that had been swallowed by oceans.

And it was then, quite unexpectedly, that the people of the planet had the visitor. It was he who was called the "scout". After the colonists spoke with him, he was regarded as a messenger of sorts.

But not everyone trusted the mysterious man. Some thought he had been a warrior, or perhaps a pirate.

But there were others who did trust him.

And even others still who thought he could be a 'messiah'.

But he had a message to deliver, and that was his purpose.

People were given the free will to choose to accompany him, or stay behind. But those who chose to stay behind, he had claimed, would experience a fiery death as the planet was destined to perish.

After the scout had come, after the people looked up towards the stars, and after the people's journey, there had been a feeling of despair that washed over those who waited for what was to come next.

For the journey that the people took had been a quest for survival. Leaving the safety of Sector B, out into an increasingly hostile, now foreign world.

The people, though, learned to trust the scout.

They followed him as he led them to salvation.

The masses of people found themselves standing in the midst of a large, sandy desert, on a planet which had become dangerous and uninhabitable. Radiation threatened from above during six months of sunlight. It had only been safe to venture out during the six months of darkness.

Half the world was flooded, and the other half was a barren desert. Forests and agriculture had slowly died off after the physical transformation of the planet took place once the rotation had slowed to a stop.

But the scout brought the people hope.

As they stood exposed to cosmic rays in a large desert clearing, underneath a rapidly lightening sky, they felt a twinge of the unknown. Dusty, sandy hills rolled along the plains around them towards the horizon. The sky was starting to turn from black to dark blue.

But they still felt safe, at least to a degree. For they didn't quite remember much before seeing the massive, dark cylinder in the sky that hovered over the dry and dusty landscape. As they looked up at the dark hovering spacecraft, the rest of the thoughts of the dying planet gradually faded away.

It was a massive ship; one that was miles long and wide, one that would travel vast distances at speeds that mankind had never been able to achieve.

EXCELLENCE
IN
FICTION

ALL TITLES AVAILABLE WORLDWIDE
FROM PARCHMAN'S PRESS